Dead Silent

An Eliza Gordon Mystery

by

Amy Beth Arkawy

For information, email **Cozy Cat Press**, cozycatpress@aol.com or visit our website at: www.cozycatpress.com

ISBN: 978-1-939816-04-7
Printed in the United States of America

Cover design by Keri Knutson
http://alchemybookcovers.blogspot.com

1 2 3 4 5 6 7 8 9 10

Dedication:

For my sister, Shana: faithful friend and ardent fan. My gratitude for all the years of reading rough drafts and cheerfully shilling plays, books and radio shows is measured in the bounty of our laughter and joy.

Chapter 1

"Talk about the naked truth," Midge Sumner said with a laugh. She raked her fingers through her auburn hair, frizzed into an impromptu Orphan Annie perm courtesy of Mother Nature. She glared at her laptop and shifted excitedly on an oversized red stool at the counter of Soup Opera, her best pal Eliza Gordon's popular eatery.

"Guess the camera doesn't lie," Eliza said, whipping out a crumpled ten dollar bill from her colorfully soiled apron pocket and depositing it in her friend's lap. She leaned her tall, slim body against the counter. "It was a burden to carry all that money around anyway," she joked, turning up the volume on the little radio. She liked the peppy oldie the local station was playing.

"You give up too easily," Midge said, quickly stashing the winnings in her Dooney and Bourke red and tan summer satchel, and returning her attention to her laptop. The *Goodship Grapevine*, the local gossip website that had the suburban hamlet of Goodship in Westchester County, some forty miles north of New York City, all abuzz was showing an old Woodstock slide show, with Jill Dondi owner of the local country market the star attraction. Figuring out just who was behind the site that had already blown the whistle on local tax cheats and adulterers had replaced the Yankees and Mets as the town's most fervent summer spectator sport. Eliza had wagered that Jill, who was one of the town's premier gossips, was, in fact, the creator. But now with this embarrassing picture, she was sure her contender was out of the race.

"I beg to differ," Eliza said, ladling out a cup of Gazpacho and placing it on a new pop-art placemat featuring Warholian styled portraits of classic stars like Bogart and Bacall, Bette Davis and Joan Crawford. Her assistant Dee Dee Danziger had created the prints for a college art project and Eliza thought they'd complement her décor of old movie posters.

"It's not *so* bad," Midge said after indulging in a spoonful.

"She was what, twenty-one, twenty-two? Everyone's pretty perky at that age." Eliza glanced at the computer screen and shook her head. "Naked as the day she was born. But still with the bouffant."

"Yeah, she was born with that hairdo. They should dig up some baby pictures." Midge laughed. "But I was talking about the soup."

"Oh. Thanks for the ringing endorsement," Eliza said. "Let's hope third time's the charm. If it doesn't sell tomorrow I'm never making it again."

"Promises. Promises," Midge joked. "Quite tasty, actually. It sort of grows on you."

"Don't you dare say 'like a fungus,' or I may just burst into tears." Eliza hauled a big vat, three quarters full of the summertime *soup du jour*, into Soup Opera's small kitchen, placing it on the center shelf of the fridge. It had been the featured soup for two days running; one more day and an inspector from the Health Department might pop in for an unwelcome visit. Eliza didn't understand people. They were smack dab in the middle of an August heat wave, with daily temps topping off in the low nineties and a frizz alert that could curl the stray hairs on a bald man's neck and still customers were eschewing the Gazpacho and cold melon soup for clam chowder, lobster bisque and black bean.

"She was a long shot, anyway," Eliza said, returning from the kitchen. She plopped onto a stool across from Midge, brushing fly-away strands of her honey-brown hair, escapees from her listless, late-day pony-tail across her forehead. "I never had Jill pegged as a cyber whiz." It was nearly eight o'clock on a Thursday evening. The last of the sparse summer commuter crowd had already strolled in for a quick take-out dinner of soup or sandwiches. Usually, Eliza closed by seven, but sometimes she'd keep the OPEN sign in the window if she was cleaning up or working on a new recipe. Tonight, she was just hanging out with Midge.

"My money's still on your brother-in-law," Midge said.

"Really?" Eliza asked, pulling off her soup and chalk stained apron.

"You do the math," Midge said, reaching for the lone jumbo chocolate chip cookie stashed under a big glass dome on the counter. "It looked so lonely." With a sheepish grin, Midge dove right in, caressing the sacred chips with her tongue. "Look, I've made room." Midge tugged on her oversized gray 'WSHP: Locally Rolled Oldies' t-shirt. She was looking svelte and healthy; her summer diet of grapefruit, grilled salmon and low-cal Cole-slaw along with regular tennis games had helped her shed nearly fifteen pounds.

"Go ahead. Indulge," Eliza said, holding out her hand for a morsel. "And it's nice to share. I have room, too," Eliza yanked at the blue and white striped oversized oxford shirt that had once belonged to her late husband.

It was true: Eliza's brother-in-law Jonas had breezed into town the first week in May(about a week before the *Goodship Grapevine* popped up on computer screens all over town), claiming his visit would be two, three weeks tops.

"He's an international man of mystery, after all," Midge said. "Is he ever leaving? Or is he back for good?"

"Don't ask me."

"You are—pardon the expression—living with the man."

"Let's just say we don't exactly have that much to say to each other." Eliza left it at that. She didn't want to go into the tension, the nonsense with those weird parties and the more than occasional sleepover guests that made going home—even to that sprawling house with more than enough rooms in which to hide—increasingly uncomfortable. Jonas was, after all, her beloved late husband Eddie's baby brother. Eliza tried to avoid confrontation. She was no longer a soap actress, and even when she had been, she tried to keep her real life drama to a minimum.

"I wonder what he's up to," Midge said. "Whatever it is, he's pretty computer savvy, isn't he?"

"I guess." Eliza liberated her long, luscious hair from the confines of the work-a-day pony-tail. "I just hope he stays."

"Really? Do tell. Does the Police Chief know?

"Don't go there. My motives are pure," Eliza said, with a laugh she hoped sounded carefree. The Police Chief was Tom Santini, who she'd just started dating a few months before. He'd also been Eddie's best friend.

"So where is our favorite law enforcement officer anyway?

"Town Council meeting," Eliza said. "But what's the difference? It's not like we're joined at the hip."

"Think I should open tomorrow's show with 'Chapel of Love?'"

"Not even close."

"Not yet, maybe."

"I'm not ready for that…and Tom, well, he—"

"I know, I know, he's an F.O.B," Midge said, using Eliza's code for Funny Old Bachelor, a term of endearment for a man over forty who's never even walked near, let alone down, the aisle. "But I've known Tom all my life, and he's smitten with you. I'll betcha he pops the question by Christmas."

"You're on. I want my ten dollars back." Eliza's romance with Tom, which had started as a flirtation last fall and had been on a sweet and slow simmer since last Christmas, was exactly what she needed right now. Eliza might have even been falling in love with Tom, but she had things to work on before she'd even consider remarrying.

For one thing, she had to get her living arrangements squared away. And that's where Jonas came in. Though she wasn't privy to just what had caused her brother-in-law's apparent change in plans—or for that matter, just why he came back after so many years away—Eliza was happy that Jonas' stay seemed to be extended and indefinite. She was using it as a nudge to finally move out of the Gordon Family Museum, the name she and Eddie had affectionately come to call his stately family homestead. She'd lived there for five and a half years, three as Eddie's wife, and two, almost three as his widow. Eliza had hoped to move out for a long while, but just couldn't abandon the home. Now if Jonas would take up residence, she could finally move out and into the little town house she'd been eyeing in the Briar Ridge Estates.

"Even money's on your nephew," Eliza said, now ambling toward the cash register. "Ethan came home from college in mid-May, right? And didn't he do an internship at Google last year?"

"I don't know. If you listen to Alex, the kid's got no ambition other than drinking, girls and driving his parents crazy," Midge said. "You waiting for me to pay for something? The cookie I'll pay for. The soup I didn't order."

"It's on the house," Eliza said with a dismissive wave. She'd actually already stashed the daily earnings into a bank envelope. She was expending nervous energy rearranging the novelty candy dispensers that offered patrons free old fashioned penny candies like Smarties, Tootsie Rolls and licorice nibs. "Think fast," Eliza said as she tossed a caramel square to Midge.

"Saboteur," Midge laughed as she fondled the coveted confection.

"One candy will not cancel out your hard work."

"You know me, I can't stop at one," Midge said, stuffing the entire candy in her mouth. "Hi, my name is Midge and I'm a junk food junkie."

"You'll be fine. Moderation, my friend. You know that."

"In my family we are not personally acquainted with the concept," Midge said, clicking on a *Grapevine* icon labeled "Hot new Pic!!" "Will you look at this?" Midge said with a healthy dollop of disdain.

Eliza scooted over to the counter and took a peek. A picture of Midge's brother's wife Poppy and Paul Hackett, the local bad-boy radio host looking rather chummy at last week's art benefit dinner radiated off the computer screen with more than a smoldering hint of sexual intrigue.

"So? It's just a friendly photo," Eliza said with forced nonchalance.

"A little too friendly," Midge said. "It'll get people talking."

"About what? They're at a party. It doesn't mean anything."

"I told Alex. I've always told him. Poppy's a delicate flower. And he's never watered her enough. And now look: he's got rot through the whole garden."

"You're a poet, Midge. Who knew?" Eliza laughed.

"You know what I mean," Midge said, her eyes rolling towards the ceiling, in both disgust and amusement. "It's never been the marriage of the century. Not that I should talk." Midge looked glum. Eliza knew her friend was thinking about her own marriage to celebrity chef Gus Delano, a renowned philanderer with bistros in both Goodship and New York City, and a hit TV show on the Eating Channel. With a shrug and a chortle Midge polished off the rest of the cookie.

The door chimes startled Eliza and Midge. Two girls—sixteen, maybe eighteen at the most—strolled to the counter. "We saw the OPEN sign," a tall, slim brunette said. She was clad in white shorts and a snug black Lady Gaga t-shirt.

"We're dying of thirst," said the other girl, a shorter, plump blonde dressed in a long denim prairie skirt and a long-sleeved red and white gingham checked shirt. She was wearing too much clothing for the weather; and the look was a tad too Amish for Goodship.

"Help yourself," Eliza said, nodding in the direction of the beverage cooler against the wall. The girls fetched their bottles.

"Jonas is so nice," the chubby girl said with a shy smile as the girls paid for their bottles of Minute Maid lemonade and Poland Spring raspberry and lime and a small sack of Smart Food popcorn hanging on a strategically placed rack near the register.

"Yes," Eliza smiled. "He is."

The girls waved and headed back into the muggy evening air.

"Excuse me?" Midge's eyebrows were affixed in an instant lift.

"She's been up at the house a few times."

"Really? Doesn't seem like his type," Midge said taking a swig from her Diet Pepsi bottle. "Is she even legal?"

"I don't know. But he has a bunch of them, once, twice a week. They always come in packs...five, sometimes ten, twelve at a time. Mostly girls a few boys."

"God, she could be Hannah's age. Did you ever see my daughter up there?"

"No, but like I said, I'm not exactly invited. Why don't you ask her?"

Midge snorted.

"She's still giving you the silent treatment over that teen tour?"

"Worse. The monosyllables."

"Uh oh."

"It's okay; I pretend I enjoy it, which of course, bugs her to no end."

"Very devious, mom."

"Yeah, well she forgets who she's dealing with. I used to be a teenager. I know the drill." Midge took another swig of Pepsi. "She'll get over it. Anyway, the SAT prep course and working half days at the Nature Center are better for her. I don't need her traipsing all over Europe with a bunch of hormonal teenagers and two negligent chaperones who are only tagging along for the free trip."

"She'll get over it."

"She'll have to. She's not earning enough. See how quickly the 'tude changes when she needs spending money."

"For what it's worth, I haven't seen her at the house with Jonas and his harem."

"Oh brother," Midge shrugged. "Charisma and stamina: a lethal cocktail."

"At least there's no booze."

"Alcohol-free parties? That doesn't sound like Jonas Gordon. Don't tell me he's Born Again or something."

"Well..."

"No... come on!"

"I don't know, like I said I'm not invited. But I walked by one night and they were out by the pool reading...or more like waving bibles."

"Oh, God, no pun intended. This is just too precious." Midge smacked her lips. "Wait 'til it hits *The Grapevine.*"

"It might not. I mean if you're right about Jonas being behind the site."

"Unless he wants it out. Maybe it's a cover for something."

"Like what?"

"Who knows with that kid? Apparently *God* only knows."

"I wish you'd tell me his deal. Eddie was always so vague." Eliza hit the candy jars, scoring a few Tootsie rolls and some licorice. Eddie had always offered sketchy stories about his brother, how he was idling with models in Milan, gambling in Monaco, playing polo in Argentina. Eddie's favorite quip: "The kid's running through his trust fund like it's burning a hole through the pockets of his tight Elvis leather pants." Eliza always retorted that such pants didn't come with pockets.

"Sorry, but you know about as much as anyone," Midge said, casually grabbing a licorice from Eliza's Humphrey Bogart placemat. "Jonas is twelve years younger than Eddie, so by the time he was old enough to get into any interesting trouble we were all at college. Then he went off to college and rarely came home. The last time I saw him...." Midge hesitated, stared down at the earthy wood floor.

"I know," Eliza said. The last time they'd seen Jonas, before the summer had been at Eddie's funeral, nearly three years ago. Eliza had, in fact, only met him twice, at her wedding and then at the funeral.

"So what's with these parties?" Midge asked.

"Dunno. He calls them personal growth workshops. He started in June. They usually run for an hour or two. By nine they're done,"

"They probably have curfews." Midge laughed, pawed a Tootsie roll.

"Then he takes off to who knows where. Probably down to the city. He comes home in the wee hours. It's not uncommon to find one, sometimes two bimbos milling about the kitchen in the morning."

"That sounds more like it. So he's up to his old tricks."

"I guess. But those parties are still strange."

"The devil has his servants," Midge shrugged, as Johnny B. Goode, WSHP's early evening deejay segued into "Devil in a Blue Dress."

"Speaking of devils," Midge said as Paul Hackett, the local lothario wreaking havoc on her brother's marriage, walked into Soup Opera.

"Burning the eight o'clock oil, ladies?" Paul Hackett, a man in his late forties dressed in a washed-out green polo shirt, baggy khaki shorts and worn out sandals, exuded a smug swarthiness that belied his burly, balding looks. When people told him he bore a striking resemblance to Tony Soprano he actually took it as a compliment.

"Cutting it close, aren't we?" Midge pointed to her watch. Not only wasn't Midge a Paul Hackett fan, she was practically his boss. Well, she and her brother owned WSHP, Goodship's local radio station. She hosted the midday show, a blend of oldies, community announcements and pithy comments and handled promotions. Alex was the General Manager in charge of sales and business affairs. He was the one who'd hired Paul, a down-on-his luck radio nomad who happened to be his old college roommate back in January. Since then, Hackett's talk show had burned up the local airwaves weeknights from nine to midnight with an incendiary explosion of politically incorrect commentary that infuriated the right, the left and everyone in between. Midge thought it denigrated the station's reputation. Alex always pointed out the ratings' spike.

"Not to worry, boss," Hackett said, leaning over Midge's shoulder. "I've got it under control."

"I'm sure," Midge said. "You can insult everyone blindfolded with your hands tied behind your back without a minute of prep."

"As long as you don't put a gag in my mouth," Hackett said. "Hit me with two, make it three Snapples, hon," he said to Eliza with a boyish wink. "I have a lot to talk about tonight."

"Help yourself," Eliza said, waving her hand toward the cooler.

"But don't underestimate me. I'm always prepping." Hackett paid Eliza for the teas and a bag of Doritos he grabbed on impulse.

"Have a good show," Eliza said, as Hackett sauntered to the door.

Hackett flubbed a few lines from "Heard It Through the Grapevine," loud and off-key, his hands motioning the chattering of gossip's teeth.

"Idiot! " Midge sniped as the chimes signaled the big mouth's exit. "He can't even get the lyrics right."

"Geez, you really have it in for the guy."

"Let's just say I can't wait for September."

"What's happening in September? I mean besides the kids going back to school?"

"We're finally getting rid of that low-rent Rush Limbaugh. But don't tell anyone. It's not for public consumption yet."

"You're firing him? I thought his ratings were through the roof."

"They are. And no, I'm not getting the satisfaction of firing his fat mouth. He's dumping us."

"Really? After Alex got him the gig."

"Yeah, well, apparently the superstar's outgrown us. Seems the snake got himself a syndication deal. He's headed to New York October one."

"So that should make you happy."

"It does."

"So why do you still looked so peeved?"

Midge was staring at the *Grapevine* photo. "I don't know. But if he's really having an affair with Poppy...I mean if it's more than a fling, then we may never really be done with that scoundrel." Midge nervously rummaged around her satchel, pulled out a half-eaten melting Milky Way bar.

Chapter 2

Eliza had been here before. Twice. She was hoping her third walk-through of 18 Briar Ridge—with Tom Santini in toe and a handful of open-housers milling about—would be the charm.

"Third time lucky?" asked Nadine Riccio, the sixty-something walking Botox ad of a real estate agent, as she tugged gently on the billowy sleeve of Eliza's blue batik blouse. "Hope you're not just here for the cookies."

Eliza laughed, waving off Lila Overby, Nadine's junior associate who was cheerfully passing around a plate of shortbreads and ginger snaps. Lila, wide-eyed and fiftyish had dreams of big commission checks filling her empty nest. She had to be an optimist, Eliza realized, to expect to make good money in the worst real estate market in years. Of course, one man's ceiling is another man's floor, Eliza noted with a wry smile. She would do quite nicely in this buyer's market. That was one reason to make her move now. She was also being prodded by Dr. Sylvan, the therapist she'd seen after Eddie passed away and who she started to see again recently to sort out her feelings for Tom.

"So, what do you think?" Eliza asked Tom as they stood by the stone-encased fireplace.

"I can see us...*you* here," Tom said, blushing. He nervously ran his fingers through his lush head of salt and pepper hair. Then he shoved his hands into the pockets of his stone chinos and stared out the sliding glass doors.

Eliza smiled. She found his faux pas endearing. For Tom, whose romantic moves were far more tortoise than hare, such a remark was revealing. Maybe Midge had been right. Maybe Tom was ready to get serious. The question for Eliza: just how did she feel about him, about becoming an *us* with another man? She was beyond fond of Tom. And there was an undeniable attraction. Of course, it was easy, as the police chief was a tall, sturdy, handsome cut of a man with sparkling azure blue eyes that undercut both his forty-three years and his important position. But the passion—that fast fire she'd felt with Eddie—wasn't quite there. Maybe you only got to have that kind of love once in a lifetime; and that's if you were truly blessed. But, as Dr. Sylvan had often pointed out, there were all sorts of ways to attain a rich, loving relationship. You just had to be open, and willing to work at it. Eliza certainly didn't want to lose whatever it was that she had with Tom. This special friendship, this growing affection for Tom had become very important to her. Even if she couldn't exactly call it love. Not yet anyway.

"Priced to sell," chirped Nadine as she joined Eliza and Tom in the kitchen. It was a far cry from the large, designer kitchen she and Eddie had created in the Gordon Family Museum, but it wasn't a mere galley either. And it was still a bit bigger than Soup Opera's epicenter. The kitchen—with a bank of new shiny appliances—opened into a comfortable dining nook, followed by the sizeable living room, which was surrounded by the sliding glass doors, opening up to a nice patio and garden.

Yes, Eliza thought, as she checked out the tiny laundry/utility room nestled between the kitchen and a small downstairs bathroom, *this two-story townhouse in a new rustic development on the edge of Goodship could be a good place to officially start over.*

"But I'd make your move soon," Nadine said, following Eliza like a clingy two year old. "Those two look serious." She motioned to a familiar young couple opening and closing the refrigerator with something less than buyers' enthusiasm. Eliza recognized the girl as Ashley Hoyns, Alex Sumner's officious, emaciated twenty-eight year old assistant, but couldn't quite place the scruffy young man. Eliza figured they were just frittering away a sultry summer Sunday afternoon. She doubted Ashley's WSHP paycheck could qualify her for a mortgage. Then again, maybe she had independent or family funds. Or a rich boyfriend, though she was pretty sure this young guy wasn't him.

"I don't know," Ashley said, slamming an oak stained cabinet. "It's a little middle-aged, isn't it?"

"Ouch," Tom chuckled.

"Too suburban prison for me, that's for sure," the young guy said as he rocked back and forth in a pair of well-worn Birkenstocks.

Eliza and Tom meandered up the short staircase and surveyed the upstairs. The master bedroom was spacious with high ceilings, hardwood floors and a big bay window which overlooked a bucolic, woodsy landscape. The upstairs bathroom was large and included what—for Eliza—could be the deal closer: an oversized sunken tub. Eliza pictured herself luxuriating, washing away her daily woes like the women in those classic Calgon commercials.

The second floor also contained a sizeable hall closet and two smaller rooms. One could be a guest room and the other could be an office or work-out space.

This really could be the place, Eliza thought as she watched Tom pace the length of the large bedroom. *He fits nicely, too,* she found herself thinking. That admission, she knew Dr. Sylvan would find intriguing. So tomorrow she'd call Nadine, finally get the paperwork in motion. She'd already called her lawyer and the bank. She could get a good deal on a mortgage. While Eddie had left her comfortably well off, much of the money was tied up in the stock market which had plummeted in the last several months. Her own small acting fortune had been all but plundered years ago by her mother's fourth husband, a self-described financial wizard who wound up perfecting his backhand at Club Fed in Allenwood, Pennsylvania. And though Soup Opera was now turning a profit, it was a paltry one and she only received occasional royalty checks for the odd TV movie. She was hoping *Family Dancing,* the sitcom she'd starred in as a child, would hit TV Land next year so she could count on a few larger, more regular checks. Still, with all the setbacks, getting the mortgage and making the payments were within her grasp. And she knew she was lucky. In a time when so many people faced hardships: job losses, retirement accounts wiped out, even foreclosures, Eliza was in a position to start afresh. And do it at a bargain price

"Go for it. The sky's the limit." Eliza recognized the distinctive baritone as she and Tom ambled back downstairs. It was Paul Hackett talking to Ashley and her young escort. Good thing Midge hadn't tagged along for moral support as she had during Eliza's two previous walk-throughs. "Remember kids, you're with me now."

Now Eliza recognized the young, scruffy kid. He was Robbie Coates, who'd worked on and off at WSHP, mostly as a part-time board operator. His big break had come in January when Hackett had hired him as his full-time producer. From the conversation, Eliza figured he—and maybe Ashley, too—would be going along for Hackett's big syndication ride. Eliza wondered if Alex and Midge knew they'd likely be losing not one but three employees in the next month.

"I don't know. I still think living in Manhattan would be cool," Ashley said as she flirtatiously adjusted the collar of Paul Hackett's white Lacoste polo shirt. "Everyone knows I've been dying to get out of this burg for years."

"We could have our own little Hollywood enclave right here in Goodship," Lila Overby cooed, greeting Tom and Eliza at the foot of the staircase.

"Mr. Hackett lives right across the way at Number 23."

"That's a real selling point," Tom snidely mumbled.

Nadine circled, shooting Lila a dagger. "Let's keep the stairway clear, please." She ushered the group—which now included Declan Rinaldi, the owner of Cheap Seats Video, a very pregnant young woman, a short, fidgety man Eliza assumed was her husband and an older woman whose short, short tennis skirt clashed with her varicose vein-lined legs, who was probably the pregnant girl's mother—back into the living room.

"So did you find anything?' Hackett asked Robbie.

"Find out what?" Ashley rubbed her bare elbow nervously.

"He knows," Hackett said, turning away from her.

"No, it's still deep undercover, I guess," said Robbie.

"Do your job, man," Hackett said, playfully punching the kid on the shoulder. "Ah, don't sweat it. I'll get the lines going with 'Who Be the B?' Just fire up the bee sounder and put some Hip Hop crap behind it and we're in business."

"Oh, now I know," Ashley beamed. "You're talking about that lamo *Grapevine*."

Eliza and Tom broke from the cluster, slipped out the large sliding glass doors and onto the patio. "This is nice," Tom said.

"It's so tranquil," Eliza said, breathing in the warm, scented summer air. The flowers—hyacinths, irises, roses—that surrounded the patio fragrantly punctuated the setting with luscious colors. Eliza could easily picture small dinner parties as well as quiet evenings for one or *two*.

She flinched as a pesky bee buzzed by. Of course it hadn't been all that tranquil in Goodship these days. Everyone was buzzing about *The Grapevine*. At least the latest item was something of a harmless curiosity: *The Vine is all abuzz about the mysterious 'B.' Flyers all over town proclaim B. The One. & B. The Best. The Grapevine can't help but ask, just who is this enigmatic B?*

Eliza clutched Tom's strong hand and they walked back inside.

"Never knock your sources." Hackett was still holding court with his protégées. "In Goodship, *The Grapevine* is bigger than *Drudge* and *The Huffington Post* put together."

"You're right," Ashley said, her hazel eyes gazing at Paul Hackett with what Eliza detected was school-girl adoration, bordering on devotion.

Declan Rinaldi waved at Eliza as he headed out the door she'd just emerged from. He looked uneasy, a little out of sorts, Eliza thought, as she caught Declan glaring at Paul Hackett as the radio big mouth gave Ashley a big kiss on her glossy ruby red lips. Eliza wondered if Declan had a crush on the girl, though Ashley was a little young for the fifty-something aging preppie. Of course, that didn't stop most guys.

"Howdy, Neighbor?" Paul Hackett joked, sneaking up on Eliza, waving a ginger snap in her face. Eliza noticed a lipstick kiss on his cheek. Apparently, Ashley had returned his amorous gesture and had left behind a little souvenir.

"Could be." Eliza smiled, snatched the cookie and took a decisive crunchy bite.

"*Carpe diem*," Nadine pounced. "You see the turnout and they're not all here for the cookies. That couple over there are ready to pop." Nadine cocked her head in the direction of the pregnant woman and her fidgety husband. The mom, Eliza guessed, was upstairs sizing up potential nurseries. A wistful wave washed over Eliza as she thought about the family she'd wanted, but never had with Eddie. Maybe, just maybe, she'd still have her chance, maybe with Tom. She was still young enough—she'd turn thirty-seven next month. *First things first,* she thought, leaving the future to sort itself out.

"There are a few vacant units," Tom said, playing hard-to-get cop. Eliza liked his supportive intervention.

"True. Number 20 and Number 36 are still available. But they're not as nice. Neither has a bay window or a sunken tub"

"I'll call you tomorrow morning," Eliza said with sudden urgency.

"First thing," clucked Nadine.

Chapter 3

The Wednesday lunch crowd feasted on more than Eliza's soup du jour: garden broccoli or her special Cajun chicken wraps. Whatever they ordered, everyone seemed to crave a side order of gossip.

"Looks like our ex-mayor will be going on a jailbird diet pretty soon," said Oscar Oleo, the hunched up turtle of a man who ran the local garage for four decades.

"You can't believe everything you read in *The Grapevine*," Bert Santini said, serving Oscar his usual: a bowl of pea soup and a buttered onion roll.

Bert was Tom's father; he was also the retired police chief who worked the Soup Opera counter two or three days a week because he liked Eliza and serving customers better than playing golf with his retired cronies.

Eliza had read the hateful entry about ex-mayor Phil Dexter earlier that morning. The gossip site heralded Dexter's possible involvement in an alleged Wall Street Ponzi scheme. Eliza hoped it was unfounded. She'd become rather friendly with Phil's wife Michelle, who provided scrumptious home-baked goodies to Soup Opera's dessert menu.

Eliza cranked up the small radio which sat on a shelf under the lopsided clock and Marx Brother's *Duck Soup* poster. Midge was on-air in the middle of "The Golden Lunch Box," her noon request hour. Sam, the new kid Eliza had hired to share Dee Dee's shifts in the fall when they both went back to college, had requested something obscure from the Electric Prunes, and Eliza wondered if Midge had found it. Today, Eliza was ignoring any bad news. She was in a blissful fog, having finally signed the paperwork yesterday that officially made her the owner of 18 Briar Ridge Lane. With immediate occupancy available, she could move in any time, and she figured she'd do so gradually over the next few weeks.

Poppy Sumner, Alex's wife and Midge's sister-in-law, slid out of a back booth and headed to the register with Georgia Rhodes, the ex-hippie owner of Knit Wits.

Everything okay, ladies?" Eliza asked.

"The shrimp salad was simply divine," Poppy said with a dramatic twinge. Tall and regal, Poppy's radiant skin, her sultry brown eyes belied her forty-six years and gave her an ageless modelesque appearance.

"Somebody's in a good mood," Lois Danziger said with a snicker as she bristled by and grabbed a stool at the end of the crowded counter.

"I'm in 'my life's a bowl of cherries' mood," Poppy said, tapping Georgia on her pink and orange tie-dyed shoulder. "And I'll be happy to give Lois the pits." She smiled her big, expensively white smile.

"Since you're so generous, why not pick up the whole tab?" Georgia offered a sly, gap-toothed grin.

"Consider it done." Poppy paid for both her shrimp salad wrap and Georgia's eggplant Panini.

As the two headed to the door, a bright yellow flyer fell from the community bulletin board that housed a catch-as-catch can collection of announcements, flyers and business cards. "This is up your alley," Poppy said with a laugh, handing the flyer to Miriam Sussman, the retired Goodship High librarian, who had just come through the door, her weathered face buried in an old hardback edition of *The Scarlet Letter*. Poppy and Georgia exited without expecting or waiting for a reply.

"B. QUIET NOW!" Miriam read aloud. "Very funny." She stashed the flyer in her large tan straw tote and proceeded to the counter without anything resembling a smile crossing her creased face.

"I certainly hope you washed your hands," Lois said to her daughter Dee Dee as the young woman placed a cup of clam chowder in front of her mother. "Too bad you can't wash *that* off," Lois snapped. *That* was the small crescent moon tattoo that Dee Dee, a twenty year old with very yellow spiky hair, had gotten on her wrist earlier in the summer, mostly to annoy her uptight mother.

"Can't you just eat at the Inn?" Dee Dee let out a sigh. Lois, a petite bird-like creature with wispy light blonde hair and a sallow complexion ran the historic Goodship Inn and had garnered a reputation as the town crank, with her steady stream of complaints lodged against everyone from newbies building McMansions to teenage hooligans vandalizing the Inn's pristine grounds.

"It's a free country. And I'm a free agent," Lois chirped.

"Wonder what class I can take to learn about a loophole," Dee Dee said, holding a Quimby College catalog. She'd transferred to the prestigious local school last spring and was majoring in art, but she also had an interest in sociology and psychology, with understanding her mother as a possible ulterior motive.

"Don't you have customers to wait on?" Lois waved her daughter away.

"I guess I can find something to do." Dee Dee laughed and headed back into the kitchen where she checked on pots of navy bean and cream of mushroom and hoped to flirt with Sam.

"Can you believe Poppy?" Lois was now talking to Miriam Sussman, who was nibbling on a tuna wrap and reading her book.

"Believe her about what?"

"Running around with that Paul Hackett character? At least if he was good looking, maybe I could understand it."

"What's to understand? Sexual attraction isn't only based on physical beauty," Miriam said, giving Lois a critical once-over. "When it comes to a woman's attraction to men anyway."

"I guess so," Lois said, self-consciously yanking on her pastel pink oversized linen shirt. The shirt, which hung on her tiny frame, swallowed Lois up; the shirt actually seemed to be wearing her. She returned her attention to her clam chowder, perhaps looking for answers in the thick, creamy pottage. A divorcée for nearly ten years—without any significant relationship since—Lois had been in Poppy's class at Goodship High. Mrs. Sussman had been a craggy librarian back then and some things didn't get better with age.

"You really shouldn't take that stuff on *The Grapevine* so seriously," Eliza said, refreshing Lois' iced tea and Miriam's lemonade.

"If you'd spend more time at yard sales instead of in front of that ghastly computer, you might find some real treasures," Miriam said proudly, waving her book. "First Edition. Quite rare...and valuable, too. And I got it at a price that would give the seller night sweats...if he knew its real value." Every wrinkle and crease on Miriam's leathery-from too many summers in the sun face seemed to crinkle with joy.

"I don't need *The Grapevine* to know what's what. Don't forget I run the area's premier hotel. I see firsthand who comes and goes," Lois said. "And anyway, a little gossip can be fun."

"Sometimes, I guess," Eliza said. She never thought Lois found enjoyment in anything. And she wondered if Lois had actually seen Paul Hackett and Poppy Sumner check in at the Goodship Inn. She figured if they'd been having an affair, they'd be more discreet and rendezvous at a hotel in another town or down in New York City. "As long as it's not mean-spirited."

"If it wasn't mean spirited it wouldn't be gossip," said Lois.

"If you engage in too much gossip it can age you five, ten years for every year you gossip," Miriam said.

"What are you talking about?" Lois asked, puckering her lips on a lemon wedge.

"I'm serious. They did a scientific study. I read about it in *The New England Journal of Medicine.*"

"I'll take my chances," Lois said, sipping her tea.

"I can see you already have," Miriam snipped.

The tension between the two women made Eliza wonder if Lois still had some overdo library books from the 1980's stashed in her back closet. And if she did, it would surely hit *The Goodship Grapevine*.

Heads turned as the chimes melodically underscored the entrance of Paul Hackett. The radio star ambled in with Ashley Hoyns, clad in a short print mini skirt and a bright red t-shirt. Eliza realized that Ashley's wardrobe, which used to inexplicably consist primarily of stodgy business suits, had become younger and more daring since her association with Hackett.

"There's a booth in the back," Eliza said, handing the two menus. "If you'd prefer a little privacy."

"That's okay," Hackett said, throwing his tattered brown briefcase on a chair at a small empty table in the center of the restaurant. "Wouldn't want anyone to have to strain their necks." He grabbed the menu from Eliza's hand and smiled that roguish, charming smile at her. "Enjoy the show," he said loudly to the crowd. "No extra charge."

They placed their orders and Eliza returned with a Cajun chicken wrap and spicy curly fries and a large Pepsi for Hackett and a small mixed green salad and Diet Snapple iced tea for Ashley. "So where's the third musketeer?" Eliza joked, noting the absence of Robbie Coates.

"Looks like I'm riding solo tonight," Hackett said, already hitting the fries. "My young serf is up in Rhinebeck for a few days."

"His mom's sick," Ashley added. The young woman apparently had a penchant for playing with Hackett's collars; this time her well-manicured fingers were adjusting the frayed collar of Hackett's hideous Hawaiian print shirt.

"Sorry to hear that," Eliza said.

"Me too, "Hackett said. "Don't tell him, but I've come to rely on that kid."

"My lips are sealed." Eliza smiled and walked over to a booth where a mom and her two 'tweens were patiently waiting for a bottle of ketchup.

By the time Eliza got back to the counter, Lois and Miriam were at it again, this time in hushed tones.

"But after what he said?" Lois was musing. "He's got some nerve."

"What exactly did he say?" Miriam asked. "I'm not exactly a regular listener."

"He called her a mad cow *and* a blubbermouth. Can you believe that? On the radio," Lois said. "I mean Jill's not my cup of tea either, but come on. Have a little compassion. Especially after being slammed by that God-awful *Grapevine*. I mean those pictures…if anyone put up naked pictures of me, I wouldn't be able to show my face again," Lois said, her face flushed. "Not that they could find any…not that there are any."

"Now it's God-awful? A minute ago you were singing its praises," Miriam said.

"Stop hiding your head in that book." Lois shook her head, as Miriam dog-eared her novel and stowed it in her large straw bag. "I may have a certain fondness for a healthy dose of gossip, but not that *Grapevine*. No one knows who's behind it, so we don't know just where they're getting their info."

"Whoever it is, wherever they're getting it, it's still gossip."

On the radio, Midge was playing "Silence is Golden" as Eliza served a bowl of garden broccoli to Declan Rinaldi and a cup of lobster bisque to Andy Ornstein, the owner of Aunt Hildegarde's Gifts, both sitting at the opposite end of the counter.

"Think Midge is sending a message to someone?" Andy asked. "Delicious." His friendly smile which seemed to set the freckles across his nose and cheeks dancing, acknowledged the bisque.

"Thanks," Eliza said, smiling at the compliment. "Who knows who Midge is trying to convince?" Eliza shrugged. She knew Midge had been upset with Hackett when she spoke with her earlier. Hackett had lampooned Jill Dondi during last night's show— describing in unflattering detail a then and now comparison of the country market proprietor's physical attributes.

"He doesn't care. He just keeps crossing the line," Midge had said.

"Well, he'll be gone soon enough," Eliza had said.

"Not before making a mess for someone else to clean up." Midge had sounded somber. "If we even can."

" Oh this is gonna be good," Dee Dee said as she swung through the kitchen door with Sam—a tall, lanky kid with a messy mop of dirty blond hair hygienically tucked under a Mets cap—balancing bowls of garden broccoli and clam chowder right behind her. "You can't miss this." Dee Dee gave Eliza a friendly nudge, stared out the window and started a countdown. "10, 9. 8…"

"What?" Eliza asked. She was still loitering at the end of the counter, her back to the window, chatting with Andy and Declan about the latest video releases and some cute knick knacks she'd spied in Aunt Hildegarde's window.

"Okay, I know some people call them kitsch, but I'm sure I could find a spot for those Alfred Hitchcock and Woody Allen bobble head dolls." Eliza laughed, realizing she'd just blown any chance of haggling.

"Really, you have to watch this!" Dee Dee was giddy with a schoolgirl laughter Eliza rarely heard emanate from her cynical young assistant.

"Okay, what…" By the time she spun around, Eliza noticed most of the patrons had dropped their spoons and forks and quashed all conversations as they braced for the pending spectacle. There was little left for Eliza to do, but lean against the counter and send up a silent prayer. Jill Dondi barreled into Soup Opera. The sixty-four year old was wearing a crazy neon yellow and purple print muumuu draped over ill-fitting yellow Lycra pedal pushers and a pair of white leather gladiator sandals. Her nostrils flaring, her head cocked for battle, her platinum blonde bouffant intact, to say that Jill was not in her usual jovial mood would be an understatement.

Dee Dee was right. There was nothing to do but watch as the events unfolded in a rapid and dramatic fashion. As Jill stormed Hackett's table, Eliza started to wonder if Midge possessed psychic gifts. Her pal had just segued into The Guess Who's classic "(She's Come) Undone."

"You have some nerve!" Jill started in, her long pink manicured fingers waving in Hackett's face. Ashley looked ashen; but Hackett's smile seemed to have grown wider. He savored both Jill's reaction and the crowd's attention, Eliza realized. "Showing your face and in broad daylight."

"Look, people." Hackett stood up, pointed to Jill. "Here she is, *larger* than life!" He let out a throaty, almost maniacal laugh.

"Too bad I forgot my garlic necklace," Jill said, trying to keep up the banter, while her eyes welled up with tears. "I didn't think vampires came out at noon."

"Bet you practiced that line all morning," Hackett said. He moved toward Jill; his attempt to give her a peck on the cheek was thwarted by the palm of her hand.

"Jill Dondi, ladies and gentlemen," Hackett said with a little bow. He shuffled to the register and Ashley briskly exited the eatery while Hackett settled with Eliza. "I'll leave you to your audience." Hackett left with a laugh and a wave.

"I'm having a pig roast and you're all invited," Jill said, regaining her composure. "I'm gonna stick that Hackett on a spit and cook him alive! And when I find out just who's behind that despicable *Grapevine* they're dead meat, too!"

Chapter 4

"No, I just told you. We're not ready…. If we're not careful this could blow up in our faces."

Eliza followed the disembodied voice. It got louder as she glided down the long, winding staircase at the Gordon Family Museum, carefully maneuvering the narrow steps in uncertain aging flip-flops. *Two, three weeks and I'll be gone,* she thought. *Finally closing this chapter.* She'd lived here long enough to expect the mixed feelings that crept up on her at the most inopportune times. Like last night when she and Tom had come back for a late snack after seeing a light fanciful movie with Meryl Streep playing Julia Child. She was in the kitchen making grilled cheese sandwiches when she found tears streaming down her face. She had to reach for an onion to conceal the memory of Eddie sitting adoringly in the breakfast nook while Eliza cooked up her very first recipe for Soup Opera. It had been an overly ambitious bouillabaisse and it turned out to be a salty, fishy, inedible disaster. But undaunted, encouraged by Eddie's unwavering faith, she'd persisted and a few months later, her new business was born.

"Don't you listen? I just said it's a no-go." The voice was louder, clearer as she walked into the study. *His* room. *Eddie.* She caught herself. That voice sounded so much like Eddie's, powerful and full of purpose. It reminded her of countless calls she'd overheard with Eddie hammering out real estate development deals, reaching across the country, around the globe, at all hours of the day and night, giving orders, guiding projects. Sitting here at his formidable mahogany desk. Or here in his chair.

Eliza ran her fingers along the back of Eddie's large burgundy leather chair. She grabbed his old moss green cashmere sweater, the one she always left draped over the chair, the one she'd often wrapped herself in late at night when she couldn't fall asleep or just needed to feel close to him. She buried her head into the soft wool, taking in Irish Spring, stale peppermint Life Savers, earth. Taking in Eddie's scent, his essence. *This I'll take with me,* she thought. The inventory of what she'd take to 18 Briar Ridge was limited. Her rocking chair and bureau which she'd had since her days in her little Astor Place apartment in New York City which were now upstairs in the bedroom she'd shared with Eddie. She'd thought about taking their big canopy bed, but after much discussion with Dr. Sylvan, realized a new bed would symbolize her openness to move on. Her readiness for this new life she was about to embark on.

"So? So, we'll just have to wait. Okay? Don't push me on this. I know what I'm doing."

The voice was clear and resolute as Eliza crossed the marbled threshold of the prized kitchen. Her head jerked back, her heart raced. She laughed at herself. Why should she be startled? It was Jonas. Of course; who else could it be? But somehow the appearance of a menacing burglar would have been less shocking. It was, after all, only seven-thirty on Thursday morning. Jonas never emerged at such a God-forsaken hour. Oh, Eliza would sometimes find one—even two—of his playmates blithely rummaging through cabinets looking, no doubt, for no-cal wheat puffs, but never the nocturnal maestro himself.

"It's not…no, I told you, it's very *quiet*. But that's just par for the course, right?"

Eliza gasped. Tall and chiseled, with wavy licorice black hair, clad in nothing but a skimpy pair of American flag shorts, Jonas looked so much like a younger version of Eddie. He glided across the cool Spanish marble tiled floor, negotiating his cell phone in one hand and Tallulah, Eliza's sleek calico, in the other. He saw her and smiled that confident, slightly crooked smile that seemed to run in the Gordon family.

"Well, yeah, sure…. Don't worry; you'll be the first to know. Bye." Jonas flipped the phone shut. "Some people. " He hit his head with the phone. "Not much going on upstairs, you know?"

Eliza shook her head, tied the sash around her blue and white striped seersucker robe a little tighter. "Morning."

Jonas nuzzled Tallulah. The cat let out a feline squeal, scratched Jonas' bare chest, escaped his grasp and slinked out of the kitchen.

"Ouch!"

"Sorry 'bout that," Eliza said, noticing red scratches on Jonas' chest. "You should put something on that." She sprung into action, milling through the utility drawer under the granite island. Beneath a Scotch tape dispenser, kitchen scissors, a package of emery boards and an endless stack of take-out menus, she finally scored a small tube of Neosporin.

"Just in case. You should put some of this on." Eliza handed Jonas the tube, averted her eyes and went about the morning motions: fetching OJ from the fridge, firing up the coffee maker, scanning the newspaper.

"Thanks." Jonas slathered on the salve, applying a more generous dose than his minor wounds surely required. "Don't worry. I've been scratched by quite a few sex kittens in my day." He laughed, again flashing that endearing smile.

"I'm sure," Eliza said, loading slices of rye into the toaster. "Can I make you something?"

"I'm not big on breakfast. Maybe some coffee."

"Oh, here's my first customer." Eliza picked up Hitchcock, her fat black cat. She snuggled the overweight bundle of love for a moment before setting out his low calorie Science Diet breakfast. Eliza couldn't deny her mutual adoration with the more corpulent of her cats. While Hitchcock loved food and people, Tallulah consumed the minimal caloric intake and ignored people with a sophisticated snobbery that made her a true feline super model.

"Okay, but this is *absolutely* it until dinner," Eliza said, placing the cat dish on the Play & Paws mat. Just as a naughty child dreaded trips to the principal's office, Eliza knew Hitchcock's wayward diet would earn her yet another admonishment from the vet. The truth was she had tried to restrict his intake, but somehow his girth continued to grow. She guessed he had a slow metabolism, not to mention a sneaky way of devouring Tallulah's leftovers.

"That one's never satisfied," Jonas said, gulping a quick glass of orange juice. "Believe me, fella, I can relate."

"You've gotten very chummy with my cats," Eliza said, smearing raspberry jam on her toast. She took her little plate and slid into the oversized cushioned seat in the breakfast nook under the window.

"Well, *we* are nocturnal animals."

"I know." Eliza took a small bite. "But today you're up so early." She motioned to the antique clock on the wall. It was just 7:35.

"Duty calls."

"What exactly is your duty…your business? If you don't mind my asking."

"It sure took you long enough."

"Well, I don't like to intrude. I figured if you wanted to tell me, you would. And anyway, we don't see each other that often. We don't exactly keep the same schedule."

"I could tell you. But then I'd have to kill you." Jonas laughed, his arms crossed around his toned chest; he leaned against the large granite island, the place where people used to congregate during the fabled Sunday brunches Eliza and Eddie had hosted.

"I knew it was a good time to hit the road." Eliza let out a nervous chuckle.

"I was only kidding," Jonas said. "I mean you know that, right?"

"Yeah, sure," Eliza said, nervously dabbing her face with a napkin.

"It's not top secret or anything. Just a little complicated. It's mostly a hassle having to deal with people in different time zones," Jonas said, now standing over her at the nook; he reached for a piece of toast.

"Want some butter and jam on that?"

"Sure. Why not?" Eliza spread butter and jam on a slice and handed it to Jonas.

"This business certainly messes with my beauty sleep." Jonas slid into the opposite side of the breakfast nook, faced Eliza.

"Good thing, some of us need more than others," Eliza said.

"Why thanks for the compliment, ma'am." Jonas flashed that famous Gordon grin again. "Eddie was lucky to have found you."

"I was lucky, too. He was so…"

"I wasn't that close to him, you know. But I know he loved you. Every time I spoke with him he sounded so happy. I could tell the way he looked at you at your wedding."

"We loved each other. Some people never find that. We were lucky."

"You know you don't have to go. He'd be pissed with me if he thought I chased you out. Of course, Eddie was always pretty pissed with me."

"Why do you say that?"

"Oh, come on. Didn't he ever complain about his black sheep baby brother?"

"No, not really."

"Really? Not even a little?"

"Well, he never referred to you as a black sheep." Eliza smiled, ran her fingers through her long, honey brown hair. "I think he just didn't know what you were doing. I guess he didn't get your lifestyle."

"Ah, he was such a straight arrow.

"That he was."

"He could be a little...I mean didn't it ever get to you? The way he was always so self-righteous, ever the protector. Didn't you feel smothered?

"No. He was so sweet with me, to me," Eliza said, gazing out the window, taking in the vast landscape that was the five well-manicured acres that made up the grounds of the Gordon Family Museum, zeroing in on that large Maple tree under which Eliza and Eddie had often spent lazy Sunday afternoons lounging, dreaming aloud, feeding each other strawberries and peaches fresh from the garden. "I know he wasn't perfect. He could be a little tightly wound, even a little self-righteous with other people. But to me he was so kind and loving. Always."

"I'm glad he was so good to you," Jonas said, reaching across with a napkin, rubbing off a small raspberry smudge from Eliza's quavering chin. "I wish he had known me better."

"I'm sorry he didn't." Eliza patted Jonas' hand as the napkin slipped from his grasp and onto the floor.

"You probably won't believe this, but I'm a lot more like my brother than anyone could ever imagine. He'd certainly be surprised."

"I wish you'd had the chance to be close."

"Obli di Obla da, as they say." Jonas looked pensively out the window. "But really, you don't have to move out. I'll be gone soon enough anyway."

"It's time. Believe me."

"I get it. Too many memories."

Eliza shrugged, shook off the salty emotion she felt well up in her green eyes. "Maybe you'll stay. It's a nice house. And it is *your* home."

"I'm not so sure. About the home part, I mean. It never really felt like home to me," Jonas said, walking to the counter; he filled cups of freshly brewed coffee from the big glass pot. "It is nice though. And it's the family albatross. Can't sell it. Not while Mother is alive…probably not after she goes either." Jonas returned to the nook, handed Eliza a steaming cup.

"Thanks." She took a sip of the aromatic brew. "Maybe Olivia will move back from Myrtle Beach."

"Doubt it. She's addicted to that golf course. She's actually nationally ranked in the over seventies, can you believe? And have you spoken to her lately? She's really working on her southern drawl."

Eliza laughed. She was feeling more comfortable. She was actually starting to like Jonas even though she still didn't have the faintest idea just what he was up to. "So maybe you will stay."

"Maybe," he said.

Hitchcock circled, pounced onto Eliza's lap, clawed at the ivory and mauve breakfast nook cushion. He was sniffing around for a snack. Already? It wasn't even eight o'clock yet. "No way, José!" Eliza nuzzled the fat cat with a defeated sigh.

The phone rang, startling both Eliza and Jonas.

"It's yours," he said, handing Eliza the cordless from the counter.

"Good morning, Soup Opera," Eliza reflexively answered.

"I'll leave you to it," Jonas said, walking out of the kitchen with a laugh.

"Sorry," Eliza laughed. "Hi, it's me."

"Are you at work? What number did I dial?" It was Midge. She sounded strange.

"No, I'm home. It's just habit," Eliza said, clearing the breakfast dishes. "What's going on? You sound funny."

"Put on the TV. News 12. Do it now." Midge spoke like a dazed automaton.

"Okay, hang on. I gotta find the remote." Eliza plopped the dishes in the sink and started rooting around for the remote. "What's going on?"

"Just put it on already!"

"Okay, okay, lady. Hold your horses." Eliza finally found the remote on the counter hiding under a Lands End catalog and the Life & Style section of the local newspaper, *The Journal News.* "Just a sec." Eliza turned on the little television perched on a small shelf nestled next to the Viking double ovens. She clicked on channel 12.

"Oh my God!" She yelled.

"Do you see it? Do you see him?"

Eliza stood there, mouth agape, staring at a file photo of Paul Hackett: his big moon face, squinty eyes and mischievous smile radiating life. A banner under the picture read: WHO KILLED LOCAL RADIO HOST? The anchor was blathering on about upcoming details, Midge was making incredulous noises and Eliza's head was swirling.

Jonas returned to the kitchen, a navy blue YALE sweatshirt now covering his chest.

"Damn it!" He stared at the TV screen, too, whipped out his cell phone, quickly punched in a number. "Looks like it's already hit the fan!"

Chapter 5

Eliza parked her green Jeep in the little lot behind Soup Opera. Before she even got out of the car, she could smell a mix of fresh cut onion grass, car exhaust and burnt Arabica beans from Joe's Bottomless Cup hanging in the stagnant August air. She was glad to see that Dee Dee and Sam were already working pots of vegetable, Manhattan clam and cream of mushroom. She handed Sam a yellow lined sheet with the daily sandwich specials: Portobello and spinach Panini, smoked turkey wrap and Cajun chicken flatbread, all selections she'd jotted down before Midge's call, earlier in the morning when the day had seemed to hold a now forgotten simplicity. Then—leaving out the few details Midge had relayed—told them the news of Hackett's demise.

"Summertime and the living is creepy," Dee Dee said, slicing red and green bell peppers with an alacrity the young woman had achieved in her year long stint as Eliza's assistant. "Well, I guess it's *deadly* for one creep."

Sam quickly quashed his hesitant laugh as his eyes met Eliza's disdainful glare. "Just write out the Specials Board," she said, handing him a fat pink chalk stick. "I'm not sure when I'll be back."

"I wonder who did it," Sam said to Dee Dee as Eliza headed back to the door.

"Were you sleepwalking yesterday?" Dee Dee let out a cynical, middle-aged sigh. "I'm pretty sure they have a prime suspect."

"Oh, right. That older lady with the weird helmet hair," Sam said. "She was real mad, but still....I mean murder?"

"Take my advice: be careful just what you post on Twitter and Face Book," Eliza said, her quick return catching her assistants by surprise. She grabbed her shabby black umbrella from the stand in the doorway alcove. *In case the weather guy was right about the afternoon thundershowers,* she thought. "You never know what can come back to haunt you in forty years."

Eliza slipped out of Soup Opera and back into the thick, muggy morning air. *So people will think Jill Dondi murdered Paul Hackett,* she thought as she walked down Pleasant Street, Goodship's main drag. *Just how did The Grapevine get those forty year old Woodstock photos of Jill, anyway?* Eliza wondered. She spied Max and Lenore Olivetti already working on two early, brave heads in the chairs at Shear Genius. At the end of the street she peered into Dondi's Country Store. She eyed the big old-fashioned pickle barrel, the hanging salamis, the kitschy wall quilts. But no Dondis. Neither Jill nor her daughter Marci had opened up yet. *Doesn't mean anything,* Eliza thought, glancing at her watch. It was just a few minutes past nine. Like most of the merchants, with the exception of Joe's, Dunkin' Donuts and the hair salon, Dondi's didn't open until at least 10:00.

There was only handful of people on the street, folks in tennis whites and golf plaids, grabbing coffee and muffins before heading to the country club or beach. Everyone seemed happy enough for a steamy Thursday morning; either they were oblivious or indifferent to Hackett's murder. As she crossed the street, heading past Aunt Hildegarde's and Odd Tots, Eliza noticed a young mother negotiating a double stroller and a mammoth Dunkin Donuts' iced coffee, teetering on precarious red leather high-heeled sandals. The sight amused Eliza at first; then something about the woman—her awkward struggle, her impractical, ostentatious shoes—suddenly saddened her, reminding her of Jill's scene-stealing moment at Soup Opera yesterday. She wondered if Jill had heard the news. She wouldn't be sorry, surely, but maybe she'd be so shocked, too shocked, to open up and face the world today. Or maybe she'd already dyed her signature platinum blonde bouffant midnight black, packed up her pink Cadillac with a lifetime supply of hairspray and headed for safer climes. Maybe Jill Dondi was, indeed, on the lam. *That's ridiculous.* Eliza actually chuckled aloud. People who make grand gestures and public spectacles are rarely guilty. *On soap operas and TV movies.* But in real life they're easily the prime suspects, and more often than not, probably culpable.

Eliza started to regret her decision to walk through town and up the hilly side streets to WSHP. She sauntered by Cheap Seats Video; Declan Rinaldi, looking preppy and normal in a flattering bright purple polo shirt, was already at his perch behind the big counter reading *The New York Times* even though the *Sorry, We're Closed* sign still hung in the window. Eliza rapped on the glass window and gave him a quick wave, forced a friendly smile. Declan returned the pleasantry and Eliza wondered if he knew. She remembered Declan didn't seem to be much of a Hackett fan when she had seen the two men at the Briar Ridge open house the previous Sunday. *God,* she thought, *so much has happened in less than a week. I bought a house; my new neighbor is dead. My new neighbor was murdered!*

Eliza could already feel perspiration drip from her forehead down to her cheeks and an unpleasant dampness clinging to her royal blue capped-sleeve t-shirt and khaki crop pants. An older man in white overalls, swinging a paint bucket, and two little girls in matching pink and yellow floral sundresses skipping along the sidewalk ahead of Eliza, were moving in blurry slow-mo like something from a Stanley Kubrick dream sequence.

Eliza ducked into Joe's Bottomless Cup. *A cool drink might help,* she thought. She did still have that big trek up to Weeping Willow ahead of her.

"Let me guess: you'll have something tall and cold," Joe Meriwether said as Eliza approached the long Formica counter looking as wilted as she felt. Joe's shiny mocha dome, he often said, was his calling card. "Coffee has made me the man I am today. I used to be an albino," he frequently joked. But it was Joe's smile, as broad as his substantial shoulders that invited people instantly in, ensuring his thirty plus years of success, allowing him to more than merely hang on in the last few years with Dunkin' Donuts across the street and Starbucks the next town over and all across the county.

"It's not just an old wives' tale," Georgia Rhodes said sipping steaming hot coffee from one of Joe's signature bright yellow oversized cups. "The hot stuff is what cools you off." Indeed, Georgia looked cool as a cucumber in a mint green smock top and faded denim cut-offs.

"Maybe, but I'll still stick with a tall iced coffee, please. House blend is fine. Lots of ice. One Splenda and a splash of low-fat milk."

"To go, right?" Joe started filling a large plastic glass with fresh brewed house blend, a concession to the portable lifestyle the chains indulged.

"Still moonlighting at the Psychic Friends Hotline, I see," Eliza joked. She was starting to feel a little better; the cool breeze of Joe's fan was reviving her.

"They'll need a real psychic to figure out who killed Paul Hackett," Georgia said.

"So you've heard."

"Some business, huh?" Joe said, adding a large shovelful of ice into Eliza's glass. "Real bad business."

"Midge must be upset," Georgia said. "They whacked him during his show, right?"

"After, I think," Eliza said, surprised people had heard the news and actually had some details, even if they were the wrong ones. Then again, that's how gossip traveled through the grapevine. God, she thought, *The Goodship Grapevine* will really have a field day with this.

"They must have a long list of suspects," Joe said, adding the Splenda and giving the drink a spin in the automatic shaker, "Seems everybody had a beef with that guy."

"You know me, never one to tell tales out of school..." Georgia's pre-amble was pre-empted by laughter and eye rolls. "Okay, you two, have your fun. But I heard Jill put on quite a performance yesterday. Right after I left. Natch. I always miss the juicy part."

"Poor baby," Joe said. He handed Eliza her arctic beverage.

"Okay, so it wasn't exactly her finest hour," Eliza said. "But people say a lot of things out of anger. It doesn't mean she acted on it." Eliza didn't even bother with a straw; she gulped most of the drink down. She was surprised at just how thirsty she had been.

"Too obvious, huh? So you're already trying to solve it."

"No, I just..."

Declan Rinaldi ambled in, looking dapper and remarkably cool in his purple polo, crisp white stone shorts and a pair of brown penny loafers without socks.

His big brown eyes twinkled behind preppy tortoise shell frames as he hummed "As Time Goes By."

"Somebody forgot to send me the memo," he said. "I mean three merchants congregating? It must be a meeting."

"It's a movement," Georgia offered with a snicker. "You know like from 'Alice's Restaurant.' Add another and we can wage a revolution."

"I don't think I'm quite ready for that." Declan said, perusing Joe's big muffin basket, his eyes darting from blueberry to cranberry orange, corn, apple spice, bran, and back to the corn. Even though he was about the same age as Georgia—mid to late fifties—the cinemaphile didn't seem to share the aging ex-hippie's liberal leanings. Eliza had never heard Declan expound on politics, but she had him pegged on the conservative side. "What goes with this?" Declan waved the large corn muffin at Joe.

"Your best bet: the Kenyan Morning Blend." Declan nodded and Joe started filling a bottomless bright blue cup with the aromatic brew.

"So what'd I miss? What's on the agenda?"

"Murder," Georgia said.

"Really? I didn't see you last night."

"Me? Don't look at me. I've got an alibi. I was playing bridge at Poppy's," Georgia said. "People will vouch for me. Didn't get a good trick all night."

"That's what you said last week," Declan said, nibbling on the crusty crown of the corn muffin. "I mean *Death on the Nile,* okay, skip it. But *Murder on the Orient Express*? Missing that is a crime. And I don't care if you saw it twenty times on TCM. You have to see it on a wide screen. With an audience." Declan was talking about the Summer Film Series he co-hosted at the Goodship Community Playhouse. Wednesdays in

August were devoted to movies based on Agatha Christie novels.

"We weren't talking about the movies," Joe said, sliding Declan's oversized coffee cup in his direction.

"No, unfortunately there's been a real murder," Eliza said.

"Really? Who? What happened?" Declan lifted the mammoth cup and took a shaky sip.

"That radio guy. Paul Hackett," Joe said.

"Somebody whacked him. During his show," Georgia said.

"*After*," Eliza said.

"What?" Declan stumbled a bit, almost tripped over his own loafers. He managed to shield his cup before spilling more than a few droplets of coffee onto the bright multi-colored tiled floor. He staggered to the big blue velvet couch by the window.

"Take it easy there, fella," Joe said, bringing Declan his coffee and a tall glass of iced water.

"I didn't know you were friends or I would have handled the news a little more delicately," Georgia said, twirling a few strands of her stringy, dishwater-brown-gray hair.

"No, it's just… I just saw him last night."

"Really? Where?" Eliza asked.

"At the station. After the movie let out. I just popped in for a few minutes. Just to give him a movie schedule. He asked for it…for a promotional plug."

"Do you remember what time it was?"

"Well, the movie let out at 9:45, so it was a little after ten, I guess." Declan took a sip of water and then splashed a little on a napkin and ran it across his clammy, ashen forehead. "I was only there for a few minutes. It wasn't a big thing, but…I just saw him and now he's dead…murdered?! It's just a lot to take in, you know?"

"I'll say," Georgia said, pursing her lips. "So we know he was killed after ten."

"*Midnight,*" Eliza said. "He was killed after his show." Eliza was a little annoyed that Georgia had already ignored her correction three times.

"See? I figured you'd want in on this one."

"No, I...I mean...."

"You're headed up there now, aren't you? You're going to the station."

"Well, yeah, but I'm just going for Midge."

"What does Chief Santini have to say about your sleuthing?"

"I'm not sleuthing," Eliza protested, "I'm going for moral support."

Joe handed her another iced coffee. "A little extra jolt to the crime-solving neurons never hurt. On the house."

"*Et tu*, Joe?" Eliza smiled, took the drink. "Thanks." This time she stuck a straw in the lid, took a refreshing sip. "Now I gotta get moving."

"Well, God Speed," Georgia said, as Eliza headed to the door. "And don't forget to keep us posted."

Eliza offered a half-hearted smile and waved.

"I'm sure Tom Santini won't be happy with her nosing around," Georgia said.

"Well, it's good he'll be looking out for her," Joe said. "This is some bad business, I'm telling you."

"God, I just saw him." Declan held his head in his sweaty hands.

*****

The iced coffee had refreshed Eliza, fortified her for the treacherous sojourn up the hilly side streets of Crescent View, Maple and Orchid Avenues. She was sure Midge had told her Hackett was killed after his show. "He was in Studio B recording a promo for tonight's show. A show he'd never host," Midge had said when she'd finally calmed down enough to speak. But then just as quickly, she'd been ushered off the phone by her brother, Alex who had said the police needed to question them. Hackett was killed in Studio B, the little studio in which they produced commercials and pre-recorded public affairs shows and specials. *Studio B.* Those silly flyers ran through Eliza's head. *B. The One. B. The Best. B. Quiet.* And Hackett mocking them, getting ready to have fun with them on his show: *Who be the B?* Only a few days ago, the town was consumed by some frivolous innocent little mystery. And now? Now Hackett was dead and everyone would become engrossed in the deadly mystery of just who killed the most controversial man in town.

By the time Eliza turned onto Weeping Willow Lane her t-shirt was uncomfortably affixed to her slim, sweaty body. When she saw WSHP's parking lot, she realized she could have saved herself the trouble and driven over. She'd envisioned a row of police cars and the whole place cordoned off by yellow crime-scene tape. Instead, she discovered one squad car and two, maybe three, unmarked vehicles (she noticed Tom's black Miata.) And nothing seemed to be taped off. As she walked down the cobblestone path up to the little red brick box building, she saw one uniformed officer guarding the entry way. His stocky build and balding pate, at first glance, suggested a middle-aged veteran was at the ready. But as she got closer, Eliza saw the young, cherubic face, ironically, of Jill Dondi's twenty-one year old grandson, Tony.

"Sorry, Ms. Gordon, but we're not letting anyone in just yet."

"Oh, well, that's understandable," Eliza said. "Do you happen to know if Ms. Sumner is in there?"

Tony shrugged. "Sorry, I don't."

Out of nowhere popped Sadie Weber, the tall scarecrow who'd commandeered the station's reception desk for forty plus years. "Just another day in paradise," Sadie said in a chipper sing song as she grabbed Eliza's arm. "They said we could go home for the day. But I wouldn't miss this for the world." Sadie practically skipped down the cobblestone path, her messy gray mop of hair frizzed into a Brillo pad, her baggy denim jumper blowing in what passed for a meager summer breeze.

"Rough stuff," Eliza said, ignoring Sadie's morbid enthusiasm. "Is Midge in there?"

"Being interrogated as we speak." Sadie's translucent blue-green eyes beamed.

"Did they say exactly how....I mean how he was murdered?" Eliza figured she might as well pump the eager rubbernecker for info while she waited for Midge.

"Oh you haven't heard yet?" Sadie moved her bony hand up to her mouth in mock shock. "He was strangled. With the cord of his own headphones."

"So the town crier has filled you in." Midge came up behind Eliza, shook her head at Sadie. Expecting to find a disheveled mess, Eliza was surprised and relieved to see Midge fresh-faced and clad in a pair of red and white seersucker shorts and a crisp short-sleeved white blouse. By her side stood her brother Alex, tall and slim with Midge's auburn hair flecked with gray and cut in a short timeless preppy style; he also looked dapper in a pair of pressed olive chinos and a maroon polo shirt.

"A little late in the game to play Top Secret," Sadie said.

"A lot of things are late in the game," Midge said with an eye roll.

"Show some respect," Sadie said. "Remember, I worked for your father."

"How could I forget?" Midge said.

"Out of respect, I'm asking you to take the rest of the day off," Alex said, grabbing Sadie's hand. "You deserve a break."

"Sure, I can take a hint," Sadie said as she skipped in the wrong direction back up towards the entrance as Ashley Hoyns, looking stricken, made her way out of the door.

"It's been a rough morning for everyone," Alex said.

"My brother, the King of Understatement," Midge said, giving Eliza the once-over. "What'd you do swim over?"

"Yeah, straight through the town swamp." Eliza self-consciously ran the damp, crumpled napkin from Joe's Bottomless she'd been clutching all morning, across her forehead. It seemed she was the only one who looked the worse for wear. "Aren't you supposed to be on the air?" Eliza glanced at her watch; it was 10:15.

"That's the beauty of the satellite." Midge motioned to the big dish on the roof. "We're letting the boys in Denver do the heavy lifting today."

"*Today* being the operative word," Alex said. "Tomorrow we're back to business as usual."

"Yes, Master."

"Do they know anything? Who did it? Who found him?" Eliza couldn't get the questions out fast enough.

"Poor Tad Cullen," Midge said, referring to the young news director. "He went into Studio B at 4:30 looking for–of all things—a pair of headphones, can you believe? And there he was, Hackett hunched over the console, his headphone cord tightly wrapped around his neck. Tad said he tried to get a pulse. When he couldn't he lifted his head and his face was white, his eyes bulging and purplish. Tad called 911, then Alex."

"God. Did you…"

"Look at him? No."

"By the time we got here the police and medical examiner were already milling about. They didn't exactly invite us in," Alex said. "They've already removed the body."

"I'm sorry. I mean I know he was your friend." Eliza touched Alex's arm.

"Some friend." Alex winced. "Still no one deserves this," Alex said, gently patting Eliza's shoulder. "Excuse me." He walked off in the direction of the parking lot just as Poppy's blue BMW was pulling in.

"Ethan was probably the last person to see him alive," Midge said in a hushed whisper. "Besides the killer. I mean there wasn't supposed to be anyone else in the building until the morning team got in around four. The overnights are automated, you know."

"Ethan, as in your nephew Ethan? Why was he here?"

"Filling in for Robbie Coates. He screened the calls, ran the board."

"Oh God, do you think he actually saw the killer?"

"Who knows? But you need a code to get into the station after hours so it had to be someone who knew it. It could be someone who works here."

"Unless Hackett let him in."

"Or her."

"They don't think...I mean they can't think Jill did this, can they?"

"Doubt she has enough upper body strength to strangle someone to death. As far as I know they don't have any suspects. At least they're not sharing the list," Midge said, fanning herself with a legal pad she was holding. "Of course I do know someone who has an in with the police chief."

"Don't go there," Eliza said, trying to soak up the little breeze Midge was manufacturing. "I doubt Tom would be too thrilled if he thought I was snooping around."

"Guess we'll find out," Midge said, nodding in the direction of the station doorway. Tom, looking sturdy and handsome in his police uniform was now walking towards them. "Oh, yeah, I forgot to mention: he's already getting some assistance." Waddling right behind Tom was Detective Fred Duckheimer, a homicide investigator from the District Attorney's office. Eliza and Midge had encountered his no-nonsense style last fall when they inadvertently helped solve another murder.

"Did you call Gus?"

"Not yet. He gets home Sunday. I figure let him eat himself silly for a few days," Midge said with a shrug. Midge's husband, Gus Delano was co-hosting a special for the Eating Channel at the Chicago Eats and Feasts Festival. "I mean what can he do anyway? Hopefully he'll do me a favor and put on a few pounds."

"Where angels go, trouble follows," Tom said with a sly smile. He gave Eliza's shoulders a playful little rub.

Detective Duckheimer shook his head, a scowl on his deceptively friendly face. *He hasn't changed much,* Eliza thought. With the exception of a few streaks of gray in the dollop of dusty blonde hair on his head and in his bushy mustache, he was the same. Oddly shaped, carrying much of his corpulent weight in his hips and buttocks, Duckheimer stretched his navy polyester pants and tight short-sleeved white shirt to their limits.

"Angels are fine, but snoops will be dealt with to the fullest extent of the law," Duckheimer said, glaring at Eliza and Midge.

"Don't worry about us," Eliza said.

"We're on our best behavior." Midge nodded. "Scouts honor." She held up two fingers, though she wasn't sure if they were official scout fingers as she had never served.

" I'm serious, ladies," Duckheimer said as he rocked back and forth in his black rubber-soled shoes, making that quacking noise that personified his name. "Dead serious."

Chapter 6

"It's just so disturbing," Eliza said with an exhausted sigh. She crossed and uncrossed her legs as she shifted on the stiff, unfamiliar dark green leather couch. "I don't know what else to say."

"It's okay," Dr. Sylvan said, rising from the large, Sienna brown leather swivel chair. She poured water from a large pewter pitcher, refilling Eliza's small clear plastic cup with the now tepid liquid. "It's okay. Just catch your breath, sit quietly for a moment or two." She smiled her generous, wise smile.

Everything was all wrong. To think Eliza had actually been looking forward to this therapy session. She'd wanted to discuss both the ambivalence and pride the 18 Briar Ridge purchase had evoked. And then there was Jonas. Her enigmatic brother-in-law's return had eased her transition, but it had also raised questions and stirred a mélange of emotions in Eliza. She'd craved Dr. Sylvan's sharp insights. But of course, Paul Hackett's murder had erased her personal agenda. *It was,* she thought, *like coming into Soup Opera and finding all the contents in the refrigerator spoiled, necessitating wiping off the specials' board and starting from scratch. A simpleton's analogy,* she thought, hoping her mouth didn't reflexively turn into a sheepish grin.

Eliza anxiously took another sip of water. She wasn't even in the right place. When she'd arrived a few minutes before six at the cavernous modern glass-encased eyesore on Route 1 on the Goodship-Caulfield border, the building known as The Goodship Medical Arts building, Dr. Sylvan had greeted her in the second floor hallway. Her office was being re-painted, the gentle therapist explained, as she ushered Eliza into a vacationing colleague's office across the hall. So now she was sitting in Dr. Abraham Saperstein's office. It seemed wrong somehow, even slightly tawdry to bear her soul in the office of another therapist, a man she hadn't even met. And this office was too formal, with a decidedly male essence: wood paneling, big, uncomfortable leather furniture, and everything washed in dark browns and greens. Eliza yearned for Dr. Sylvan's familiar, cushy nubby oatmeal colored chairs, her soothing pale pink walls, her hypnotic Matisse print. How she longed for an entirely different conversation.

The session was more than half over and all she'd done was ramble on about Hackett's murder: Midge, Jill, Tom, Detective Duckheimer, the whole sorry mess. "At least Jill opened up as usual and wasn't arrested. I mean, not yet. No one has. I mentioned that already, didn't I? I mean she didn't...I don't think she could have done it considering she's a bit flabby and not exactly young...." Eliza stopped herself, looked at Dr. Sylvan. She didn't want to hurt her sixtyish, therapist's feelings.

"Guess that puts me in the clear, too," Dr. Sylvan said with a warm smile.

"I'm sorry." Eliza reached for more water.

"For what?" Dr. Sylvan's luminescent blue eyes always drew Eliza in with kindness and wisdom. Her presence, her silver hair cut into a youthful, flattering pixie style and her earthy clothes like today's boxy brown print smock top and tan linen pants conjured a motherly aura. Dr. Sylvan had certainly been more maternal than Eliza's own mother, Margot, had ever been.

"I'm just…I don't know why I'm so upset, I guess."

"Well, it *is* upsetting to know someone who was murdered. And it did *just* happen," Dr. Sylvan said with a reassuring nod.

"He was going to be my neighbor. You know that, right? I mentioned it, didn't I?"

"Are you missing the neighbor you'll never have?"

"What? No. I mean I never thought of it that way. I didn't really know him….I didn't really like him." Eliza bit her lip. "Not to speak ill of the dead."

"That's okay. You can't like everybody. And you don't have to like him just because he's dead."

"Not too many people liked him," Eliza said, nervously twirling a few strands of her honey-brown hair. "Guess they've got a lot of suspects."

"Do you think trying to solve the murder will bring you closer to Tom?"

"I don't know. I mean I'm not playing amateur detective or anything. But I know he'd rather I stayed out of it. So it probably wouldn't be that great for us."

"Perhaps that's what you want." Dr. Sylvan raised her gray penciled-on eyebrows into a quizzical arch.

"No, of course not."

"Are you sure? Maybe the investigation is just another excuse to put up a wall, a way to keep the relationship at a safe stand-still."

"No. I mean how could I have put up this wall? It's not like I killed Paul Hackett."

"Of course not, but now that he's dead and there is a murder investigation, it may be a convenient distraction."

"You mean subconsciously I'm looking for something to sabotage things between us?"

"You tell me."

"I don't think so. I really don't. Especially since I told you, I'm not playing detective. I'm just upset." Eliza could hear the defensiveness in her own voice as the words poured out in a rapid self-righteous succession. "A man in town was just murdered. You yourself just said it was normal to be upset."

"Okay. You have every reason to be upset. But I think if we—in what little time is left—tried to re-direct our energy to something that directly affects *your* life— we might be able to gain a little perspective. Why don't we talk about the new house, the move?"

"Okay, maybe," Eliza said, tentatively.

"Are you excited you *finally* committed to moving on?"

"Yes, I guess so."

"When are you planning to move in?" Dr. Sylvan shifted in the Sienna brown leather chair, rested her right hand on her chin, looked attentive, concerned. Eliza guessed she didn't love the proxy room either.

Eliza shrugged. "In the next few weeks. The inspection is Tuesday. And I still have to arrange for the movers…not that I have that much furniture to haul over."

"You're still getting a new bed, right?"

"Oh, yeah, I still have to go shopping for the bed."

"You haven't even *started* looking yet?" Eliza detected a hint of disapproval in the therapist's voice.

"How long can it take? It's just a bed," Eliza said, shifting again, trying to find a comfortable position. Thank goodness she'd gone home earlier to change out of her swamp clothes(*otherwise*, she thought, *she'd be forever affixed to this overbearing couch, stuck in some sort of a psychotherapeutic vortex, soaking up other people's problems*). But somehow the cool, comfy aqua sundress she'd changed into didn't match the décor. "I'll go soon. I will. Maybe even this weekend."

"Why do you think you're stalling?"

"I'm not," Eliza said, reaching for the glass of water she'd already emptied three times. "I wonder if they'll find anything at the house."

"You're worried about the inspection?"

"What? Oh, no. It's on Tuesday, I mentioned that right? It should be fine. It's a new house."

"So what are you worried they'll find?"

"I just wonder... uh...well, to be honest, I guess I wonder if the police will go looking for clues at Hackett's house."

"I think we should stop now," Dr. Sylvan said, stiffening, pursing her coral-coated, aging lips. She looked at the little clock she kept facing her on the small oak table next to the big, swivel chair. "You're obviously pre-occupied. Maybe by next week, we can get back to our real work."

Chapter 7

By Friday everybody was cooking up a theory. From ex-wives to angry listeners, the list of people who wanted to see Paul Hackett dead seemed endless. *The Goodship Grapevine* even ran a snarky Top Five Motives for his murder: *5. Fatal Fashion Sense, 4. Deadly Humor, 3. Lecherous Libido, 2. Rabid Rants, 1. Toxic Tongue.*

"It'll come down to some dame," Oscar Oleo said as he slurped up his daily pea soup. It was already after two, the lunch crowd had pretty much petered out when the curmudgeon came in complaining about an emergency repair. "Mark my words: if you want to solve this thing look at Number 3."

"I think we'll let the police handle the investigation," Eliza said, barking out the party line Tom had made her recite last night over dinner. Still, while Ethan Sumner was in the entry alcove chatting on his cell phone, Eliza was fixated on Midge's nephew's laptop, captivated by that list.

"Sounds like you rehearsed that line," Oscar said, lapping up soup residue with what was left of his poppy seed Kaiser roll.

"Don't provoke the woman, Oscar," Bert Santini said as he sidled next to Eliza behind the counter. "I mean if you want to make it to lunch tomorrow."

"Oh, I'll make it alright. That is if another yahoo doesn't overheat his car." Oscar snorted.

"I wouldn't be too quick to point fingers, Oscar. Didn't you call Hackett the other night? And I quote:

'Someone ought to take you out to the shed and give you an old-fashioned whoopin'.' Bert laughed, ran a rag across the counter.

"I did. So? "

"So, you just put yourself on the suspect list."

"I'll take a number. He got what was coming to him. For what he said about Jill. And all women. So disgusting. All that graphic talk. I couldn't repeat such crass rubbish in mixed company for a million dollars." Oscar blushed as he glanced up at Eliza.

"Appreciate the chivalry," she said with a kind smile.

"Really, you heard him. The way he went on and on about Angelina Jolie. I mean, okay, so she's a kook with all the tattoos and Hollywood fetishes. But she's good to so many kids. And her dad played the Pope, for Christ's sake."

"Amen!" Bert gave Eliza a wink.

"Laugh if you want. But he was a blight on the airwaves. I told Midge and her pompous brother, too. Told 'em I'd take my ads off the air."

"I didn't know you advertised on WSHP," Eliza said.

"I don't. But if I did I'd have yanked every last commercial."

"I'm surprised they didn't fire him right there on the spot," Bert said.

"And all that stuff about the president. Never anything positive to say. Negative, inflammatory rhetoric. All nasty noise."

"Well, that's what these guys do on the radio. They try to rile up the people on their side."

"Side? He had no side. A real phony. Said the same crap about the last president, too. Doesn't like anyone. Except Nixon."

"Really? Why Nixon?" Eliza was still glancing at Ethan's laptop.

"Who knows? Probably because he was a paranoid nut. And he dug us into China."

"And he liked to tape every conversation," Bert said.

"Right," Eliza said, wondering if maybe, just maybe, Hackett had taped a conversation with his killer. On the very night he was murdered.

"Good riddance to bad rubbish," Oscar said as he shuffled to the register. Bert handled the exchange. "It may not be a very Christian attitude. But let God do the forgiving. For both of us." Oscar meandered out the door. "Go ahead, Chief, put me on the list. It'd be an honor."

"Another Oscar-winning performance," Bert chuckled.

"Ah, so that's why you come in." Eliza laughed. "For the impromptu drama."

"Among other things." Bert smiled. "I think I'll take my leave, too," Bert said as he deposited Oscar's contribution into the daily coffers. "Don't think you'll be needing me anymore today."

"Okay, Bert. Thanks. See ya next week."

"If not before." Bert walked to the door wearing that sunny Santini smile.

Eliza doubted Oscar was Hackett's killer. For one thing, he was too openly passionate about it and like Jill; Eliza figured he'd be too obvious. Anyway, he was even older than Jill. She couldn't imagine that little, hunched up old man—no matter how incensed he became—strangling Hackett. If he'd wanted to really kill Hackett for shooting his mouth off, Oscar would have used a gun. And though he may have been a coot, he wasn't crazy. Only a crazy person would kill someone because they didn't like his radio show. Normal people might call in or write letters. Or simply change the station. But they wouldn't kill the shock jock.

But if it did come down to *some dame*, as Oscar so delicately put it that could mean Alex Sumner, and maybe even Poppy could be suspects. Eliza was pretty sure by the way Alex had reacted yesterday when she had called Hackett his friend that Midge had been right: Hackett and Poppy were engaged in some sort of hanky-panky and Alex obviously knew about it. But would he be mad enough to kill Hackett? Or what if Poppy had tried to call the whole thing off and got into some sort of violent mêlée with Hackett? Even Ethan could have done Hackett in had he known about the fling between the big mouth and his mom. He had the opportunity, for sure. But, really, did the kid even know? And even if he did, Eliza doubted he'd go that far. Of course, Hackett was notorious for his flings, not to mention a string of ex-wives, so there had to be a strong A-team and a deep bench of suspects who could have killed Hackett over his *lecherous libido* alone. Not to mention the other four motives. Well, three. While it was true Hackett's slovenly appearance and disastrous collection of print shirts may have offended some people, Eliza doubted anyone would kill him over his wardrobe.

Ethan returned to the counter, lurching his tall, scrawny body frenetically as he flipped his cell phone shut. He looked upset, his wide chocolate brown eyes pinched into reddened, sleep-deprived slits. He looked pasty as he pushed by Eliza. She felt for the kid. He looked like he'd seen a ghost. Actually, he almost had. He was probably the last person—besides the killer—to have seen Paul Hackett alive. "Excuse me for a sec," he said as he took quick control of his laptop keyboard. With series of quick clicks, Ethan's expression grew even more ominous. "Damn. So, it *is* out. But how?"

"What's out? What's wrong?"

"See this?" Ethan slammed his hand onto the screen. Eliza peered over his shoulder, viewing something titled "HOT BUZZ."

Silently they both read the item: *Just who or what is V.O.S? The answer may just hold the key to solving the Paul Hackett murder case!*

"What's that about?' Eliza asked.

"My father will freak. The Chief will be pissed."

"Why?"

"They'll think I tipped off *The Grapevine,*" Ethan said, shaking his head. "But I didn't. I swear it. It wasn't me." By his reaction, Eliza figured Ethan was also out as the webmaster of the infamous site. But if he was behind it the kid should seriously consider an acting career.

"But you know something right? You know what V.O.S. is?"

"No…but…" Ethan stopped himself, looked around the restaurant, making sure no one was listening. There were only a few scattered patrons left: a woman in a back booth who'd spent the better part of the afternoon nursing a chicken Caesar wrap and reading a novel, and a young couple at a corner table, fondling each other with French fries and sugar packets; all seemed safely pre-occupied. Still, Ethan lowered his voice and walked Eliza into the entry alcove.

"So what is it? You obviously know something."

"I don't. Not really. But it…V.O.S. was written on the studio window…in red lipstick, I think."

"You…I mean, the police think the killer wrote it? After killing Hackett?"

"I guess."

"They think it's the killer's initials?"

"I don't know. I guess. But the thing is…well, not that many people knew about it. They didn't want it to get out to the public yet."

"Right." Eliza nodded. "The police always try to keep a few details out of the press, hoping the killer will slip up or a witness or someone who knows something will come forward."

"Yeah, well the only people who knew about it were Midge and my dad and the morning guys, Tad and Dandy Dave. And me and my mom because she came with me when I went back to the station to talk to Tom and that Duckhead guy."

"Detective Duckheimer." Eliza smiled.

"Right. Duckheimer. Anyway, I saw V.O.S. and asked about it. Both Tom and Duckheimer said it was 'expressly *NOT* for public consumption.' They told me to keep it under my hat."

"So you did, right? Even though you're not wearing one."

"Ha ha." Ethan smirked, reflexively ran his fingers through his shaggy, signature Sumner auburn hair. "My dad even gave me a big speech about it last night when he got home. Now I'm sure I'll be their chief suspect."

"Not necessarily," Tom snickered as he came through the door.

"Pretty sneaky, Chief," Eliza said, giving Tom a playful slap.

"Listen, lady, if I didn't have bigger fish to fry, I could haul you in for assaulting an officer," Tom said, suppressing his bright smile.

"So you have us under surveillance?" Eliza chuckled as the three walked back into the restaurant proper.

"Some surveillance. I mean you were loitering in a very public place." Tom laughed as he mounted an oversized red stool. "Take my advice: next time you have a covert conversation, don't do it in the entry way."

"Point taken," Eliza said, slipping back behind the counter.

"I didn't call it in," Ethan said, giving his laptop one more glance before logging off. "Or e-mail it in." He pointed to the screen. Eliza and Tom peeked at the big, bold banner: *GOT A HOT TIP? SEND IT NOW TO: HOTTIPS@GoodshipGrapevine.com.*

"Don't worry," Tom said, shaking his head. "You weren't the first person I thought of."

"So who do you think let it…the V.O.S….out of the bag?" Eliza asked.

"I don't know but your Aunt Midge has the biggest mouth in the family." Tom winked at Ethan.

"Tom!" Eliza protested with a smile.

"Relax. I'm not saying it was her. But it's out now and we'll just have to deal with it."

On the radio Midge was just coming out of a commercial break. "Sunny and sizzling hot…temps topping off in the low nineties…so behave or you'll wind up breaking rocks in the hot sun….here's the Bobby Fuller Four on AM 990 and 99 FM, WSHP's locally rolled oldies."

"I rest my case." Tom laughed.

"Come on, that's just a joke. She's just doing her show."

"I know. But don't forget what we talked about last night."

"How could I?" Eliza could feel a lecture coming on and, quite frankly, she wasn't in the mood. People had always thought Eddie could be bossy. But not to her. Tom was another story. The one thing that really irritated her was when he went into his sanctimonious fatherly tone mode.

"Remember Detective Duckheimer is watching."

"Of course," Eliza said, restocking napkins in the counter dispensers. *So let the Duckhead, as Ethan had called him, and you too, Chief for that matter, watch.* She wasn't doing anything illegal or even immoral. It was, Eliza reasoned, her civic duty to figure out who the killer might be.

The woman who'd spent most of the afternoon nestled in the back booth finally made her way to the cash register, clutching a well-worn Mary Higgins Clark paperback.

"Everything okay?" Eliza asked.

"Oh, yes. Quite lovely," the woman, a pretty flaxen-haired thirtyish waif with magnetic cornflower blue eyes said. She handed Eliza a twenty dollar bill. "Keep the change."

"Really? The tab's only $10.50."

"I insist," the woman said. "For the courtesy. For the booth rental."

"Well, thank you. That's very generous."

The woman smiled and turned to Tom. "I think you're looking for me," she said, holding out her hand. "I'm Victoria Salinger."

"Oh, yes, Ms. Salinger. I'm glad you came to town," Tom said as he shook her hand.

"My pleasure," Victoria said. "By the way, in case anyone is wondering, my middle name is Odette." She scanned the expressions on the faces of Chief Tom Santini, Eliza Gordon and Ethan Sumner. They were stone-faced, but were surely working it out in their heads. Could Victoria Odette Salinger be the V.O.S. in question? "And for the record, I have an alibi."

Chapter 8

After negotiating Midge's wayward serve, not to mention the muggy Saturday morning weather, Eliza feasted on croissants and speculation at the Goodship Country Club café.

"I thought Duckheimer would pop a blood vessel," Midge said, liberally applying a coat of blackberry jam to a mammoth croissant. "He practically accused me of leaking that V.O.S. business to *The Grapevine.*"

"I bet," Eliza said, refreshing herself with orange spiced iced tea and the shockingly cold air conditioning. "Tom wasn't much better."

"I didn't, you know." Midge swabbed a glob of jam from her chin and slurped it up. "Mmmm…can't help myself. It's soooo good."

"It is," Eliza said, nibbling on her croissant without yet adding jam.

"I wish I knew who called it in. It's got to be someone from the station. I'm starting to think someone from the station is actually behind *The Grapevine,* too."

"Why? Who do you think it is?"

"I don't know. It's just a hunch," Midge said, reaching in the bread basket, tearing off a hearty piece from her second croissant. "I wish I could find a way to pin the whole thing on Sadie Weber."

"Come on," Eliza laughed. "What do you have against her? I mean I guess she can be a little annoying…"

"A little?"

"She's not that bad. And she's been at the station forever. She's a fixture."

"That's the trouble. She's been there forever. And she's been annoying me for years. Anyway, she doesn't have the savvy or the drive to start the website. But she *is* nosy and nervy enough to call in the tip."

"Unless…"

"Unless what?"

"Oh, I don't know. Did you ever think maybe it was a police source who called it in?"

"Then it'd have to be Tony Dondi," Midge said with a laugh. "I don't think Duckheimer has much use for the press." She eyed the bread basket, contemplated another croissant dive.

"You're right. And Tom wouldn't dare go against the Duckhead's orders."

"Do I detect a little dissension?"

"Just a little." Eliza gave in and spread some jam on her croissant, took a big, juicy bite. "Oh, did you hear V.O.S. may have been in Soup Opera yesterday?"

"Really? You've been holding out." Midge pulled her big lilac upholstered chair closer to Eliza's, anticipating hushed tones.

There really wasn't any need for whispering. The café was surprisingly under-populated for a weekend morning. The women guessed a lot of folks were spending one of the remaining summer weekends in places like the Hamptons, Bar Harbor or Nantucket. Their table had a wonderful window view of the club's pristine golf course. Their nearest neighbors, a middle aged foursome clad in clashing plaids, were three tables away.

"I don't know if she is *the* V.O.S., but she has the initials. And she didn't seem afraid to admit it."

"Keep talking. Spill it already, girl."

"Victoria Salinger. Hackett's latest ex-wife."

"Wow. What's the *O* stand for?

"Odette, I think she said. Anyway, she spent the better part of the afternoon nursing a sandwich and reading—of all things—a murder mystery."

"No kidding."

"Yep. And then Tom came in and she turned herself in."

"He arrested her?"

"Well, no..."

"I guess I would have heard *that.*"

"But Tom apparently called her and she came to town...voluntarily it seems...for questioning."

"So?

"So what?

"Details. Like does he think she did it? Did she kill Hackett?

"Dunno. *She* said she has an alibi."

"Well, what would she say?" Midge poked around the bread basket, ripped off another healthy hunk of croissant. "So what does Tom have to say?"

"Nothing."

"Didn't you go to dinner with him last night?"

"Yeah. At Peabody's. Let's just say: the burgers were juicy; the details were not." Eliza vigorously smeared blackberry jam and orange marmalade all over her croissant. "The police chief is rather tight-lipped."

"So he wants you to stay out of it. So what else is new?"

"Nothing. But it sure makes things awkward between us."

"He'll get over it."

"Maybe. But maybe I subconsciously want the rift...

At least, that's what Dr. Sylvan thinks."

"Dr. Sylvan?" Midge rolled her eyes. "You're still seeing her?"

"You're the one who recommended her."

"I know. But that was a few years ago. I mean, okay, she was helpful when Gus was involved with the one who dare not be named." Midge was referring to a fling Gus had had with a TV reporter named Darcy Danube a few years before Eliza had married Eddie and moved to Goodship. That indiscretion particularly stung Midge since the woman was regionally famous. "But after a while, she seemed to get pretty impatient with me. Almost like she was bored."

"Yeah, sometimes she seems a little impatient with me, too."

"That's not a good trait in a therapist," Midge said, eyeing the lone remaining croissant in the basket. "And it can't be too good for business either. I mean Woody Allen's been in therapy for what? Fifty years?"

"Yeah, but he's probably gone through a dozen therapists." Eliza laughed. "Anyway, I figure when she gets impatient it's for my own good. To give me a swift kick in the ass."

"Here comes trouble." Midge tapped Eliza's wrist, cocked her head in the direction of the café entrance. A blue and white seersucker toothpick with Ashley Hoyns sunken face and golden-tinted coif meandered towards their table. By her side was WSHP's morning DJ, "Dandy" Dave McKenna, a tall, paunchy man in his late fifties with sparse gray hair and a well-groomed salt and pepper beard. Dave, dapper in a pair of light blue shorts and bright yellow polo shirt, exuded a game show host smile as he glad-handed a few fans scattered about the restaurant.

"She sure has a way with the older guys," Eliza whispered.

"Good thing she's too *old* for Gus."

Eliza's laugh quickly morphed into a genial smile as the pair approached the table.

"Slumming?" Midge asked.

"Hi," Ashley offered with an inappropriate titter.

"Just seeing how the other twenty percent live," Dave said in his confident radio baritone.

"Well, judging from this dwindling crowd, it's more like the remaining ten percent." Midge stood up and waved her arms at the meager assembly.

"We're actually here to meet with Trip O'Dell," Dave said, scanning the restaurant. "We need to finalize the logistics for next weekend's remote." Dave was talking about the big Labor Day Weekend Blow-Out Blitz that WSHP hosted every year, featuring remotes from various local sites including the country club, a popular dockside restaurant called The Rusty Anchor and at least one local car dealership.

"Not that anybody's in the mood for anything," Ashley said, rummaging in her oversized navy and white canvas tote bag.

"Well, the show must go on," Midge said without even a hint of sympathy.

"We have the broadcast blocks broken down." Ashley reluctantly pulled out a folder filled with a schedule grid of DJ names, days, time slots and locales.

"This looks good. I'm impressed," Midge said, surprised at the organization. Even after all these years, the WSHP operation was always a little catch-as catch can, with things being done on the fly and almost always at the very last minute. Say what you will about Ashley; at least she was officious.

Midge handed back the folder. As Ashley tucked it back into her bag, a torrent of items toppled out of the bottomless satchel and onto the black and white shiny café floor. Dandy Dave and Eliza helped Ashley gather up a small cosmetics case, a packet of Kleenex, a cell phone, an I-Pod, rolls of wintergreen and peppermint Breath Savers, some loose change and a "Hackett

Hacks It…Weeknights 9-midnight on WSHP" bumper sticker.

"Sorry…. Thanks," Ashley said as she crumpled the bright red, yellow and black memento and quickly stashed it in her pocket. "We have to go, Dave." Her anxious eyes, the color of coffee gone cold, pleaded with the morning disc jockey.

"Yeah, I guess we do." Dave bailed her out with a quizzical smile. "See you later, ladies."

"Indeed you will," Midge snapped.

"Bye," Eliza said. "Wait a sec." Eliza was back on the floor, grabbing a stray lipstick tube that had rolled under the table. But by the time she'd emerged, returning to her seat with the errant item, Ashley and Dave had already departed.

"Going, going, gone." Midge laughed. "That girl sure is a strange one. Always thought so."

"Scarlett Nights," Eliza said, opening the lipstick. "It's a very distinctive shade."

"Looks familiar," Midge said, glancing at the tube. "I've seen it before."

"Yeah, on Ashley's lips." Eliza laughed.

"And someplace else," Midge said, her hazel eyes widening to stunned saucers.

"Where?"

"On the window of Studio B."

Chapter 9

Eliza was too riveted to Midge's glossy revelation to regret leaving the jeep in the lot behind Soup Opera. As Midge played NASCAR in her silver Volvo wagon along the winding back roads, Eliza pumped the lead foot for details.

"You don't really think Ashley did it. I mean look at her. She's a twig. "

"Don't let that Olson Twin-Kate Moss façade fool you. I've seen that girl in the gym. She can bench press three times *my* weight."

"Even so..." Eliza laughed. "I mean she adored Hackett. You saw how she followed him around."

"Maybe....but...oh, look at this grandma." Midge had to suddenly brake behind a late model white Toyota Camry with the audacity to follow the forty-five minute speed limit on Rocky Trail Road. They were headed to the Nature Center to drop off Hannah's SAT prep book before Midge deposited Eliza back at Soup Opera to supervise the Saturday lunch service.

"Take it easy," Eliza said. "We'll get there." Eliza hated when Midge drove; her antics were only compounded by her clean driving record. Midge admonished twitchy back seat drivers that she had nary a speeding ticket or accident to her credit. Not yet anyway.

"I know. But it's no fun if you have to crawl." Stuck behind the Camry in a no passing one lane stretch, they were now going at a rate Eliza could live with; one that irritated Midge.

"So getting back to Ashley."

"Oh, yeah. You know she was at the station Wednesday night."

"You're kidding."

"Nope. Ethan saw her. Said she and Hackett had an argument too."

"Really? Does he know what about?"

"Not sure. But he heard her call Hackett a 'lying scumbag.' Then she left in huff."

"Wow!"

"I figure Hackett probably told her he wasn't taking her with him to New York when he went for his big gig."

"That is big. Did Ethan tell Tom...or Duckheimer?"

"Yeah, I think so."

"And the lipstick. Are you sure it's hers? If it is, what's with V.O.S.? Would Ashley try to frame his ex-wife? Would she even know her name, her initials?"

"Whoa. What are you auditioning for an interview show? We happen to have an opening."

"Not me," Eliza laughed. "Maybe you should consider Ashley."

"Well, still waters run deep. And that girl is ambitious. And tightly wound."

"Sounds like she's got the makings of a talk show host."

"Let's see how it plays out."

"Well, I mean if she doesn't turn out to be the killer."

The Camry turned into a driveway and Midge hit the accelerator as she made a jarring turn at the junction of Rocky Trail and Babbling Brook Lane.

"Easy." Eliza pressed her right tennis sneaker into the plush maroon carpet, slamming on the imaginary emergency brake.

"Oh brother." Midge rolled her eyes as she zoomed by the McCracken Stables and Wilby's Fresh Fruits & Veggie Farm. "You and Gus...a couple of closet grandmas. Tell me, what's the point of driving if you can't let loose?"

"I don't know. Maybe getting to and fro in one piece. That works for me."

"I'll get you there. I always do." Midge turned into the Goodship Nature Center's entrance, zipped up the long curvy drive and into the barren parking lot. "You have arrived, Your Majesty. And in one piece as per your request." Midge snorted and clicked open the automatic locks.

"Thank you, Jeeves." Eliza laughed and took a deep breath as she quickly exited the wagon. She was surprised to find only three other cars parked in the large gravel oval on a Saturday morning.

"Looks like everyone skipped town."

"Interesting choice of words," Eliza said as they made their way from the lot to the little wooden hut that housed the information station where they would presumably find Hannah on duty. "I wonder if the killer is still in town."

"Why would he—or she—want to stick around?"

"I don't know. But a lot of killers can't help themselves. Like they have to return to the scene of the crime. It's a compulsion."

"You *have* been listening to Sunny Sylvan."

"Never mind Dr. Sylvan. Tell me you don't want to solve this thing"

"Oh, you know I do!" Midge gave the hut's inexplicably aluminum door a vigorous push.

Hannah—her curly auburn hair hanging like a shabby umbrella over her laconic teenage face—sat behind the long black granite desk, her forest green Nature Center apron draped sloppily over her anemic frame. "Why are you here?" she snapped as Midge and Eliza approached.

"Believe it or not, it's a mission of mercy." Midge waved the SAT Prep book.

"Oh, right." A blotchy pink puddle crawled across Hannah's cheeks.

"You left it on the kitchen table."

"Okay…thanks," Hannah grunted as she rearranged the visitor cards, already neatly stacked in a little wooden rack next to the desk.

"So happy to be of service," Midge said.

"Okay then…. Bye."

The hut door opened and Hannah nodded as an odd looking young man walked in and started watering the lush plants that filled the little office. Midge and Eliza exchanged incredulous glances. The man—probably in his late twenties or early thirties—didn't utter a word. He was tall and lean with a punkish haircut dyed a vibrant blue-black. He sported a purple kimono over slim black leggings; his face was nearly kabuki white with a heavy application of black mascara known lately as "guy liner," thanks to a popular contestant on *American Idol.*

"What? Are you waiting for an invitation to leave?" Hannah snipped.

"That won't be necessary." Midge looked crestfallen; her hazel eyes drained of their levity.

"I have to get back to the restaurant anyway," Eliza said with a listless shrug.

"It's not like I don't have better things to do myself," Midge said.

"So go do them," Hannah said; her eyes followed the strange young man as he continued his horticultural duties.

"I will." Midge walked back to the aluminum door. As she gave it a push, she turned her head back towards

Hannah. "Start cracking that book. I'm looking for perfect scores."

"Keep looking," Hannah muttered as Midge and Eliza finally left.

*****

The ride back to town was excruciating. Midge was silently fuming and driving like a runaway bride with a caravan of wedding planners and irate in-laws on her tail. "Reach in my bag, will you?" Midge said as she zipped through a yellow light at the intersection of Wild Orchid and Weeping Willow. "I'm pretty sure I've got a Snickers or something in there."

Eliza pawed through Midge's Dooney and Bourke red and tan satchel. "The only thing I see is a Twixt."

"Sold!" Midge held out her hand. "I don't even care if it's melted."

"It looks okay." Eliza unwrapped the candy, slipped one half of the crunchy wafer into Midge's desperate hand.

"Thanks." Midge shoved a big piece of the candy into her mouth. "I'm just gonna swing by the station for a sec."

"Uh…okay." Eliza glanced at her watch. It was almost eleven. The lunch crowd would start trickling in and she wanted to make sure Dee Dee and Sam had everything under control. Of course, judging by the sparse crowds she'd seen at the club and nature center, she suspected it would be a light day.

"We don't have to go in. I just want to see if the station van is still in the parking lot," Midge said, her hand out for her second Twixt wafer.

"Pace yourself." Eliza laughed as she dropped the candy into Midge's chocolate-stained palm. "Why wouldn't it be there? You think someone stole it?"

"Yeah, Miss Marple, that's what I'm afraid of." Midge laughed as she turned into the WSHP lot. "Oh, good it's gone."

"So, how is that a good thing?"

"It means the new kid hauled it out to the beach and is already handing out bumper stickers and beach balls… God, we still have a bunch of those to unload… I mean unless someone stole it and is cruising around town in that eyesore."

"Oh, yeah, I guess you're right." Eliza laughed. She realized the big shiny red van with the neon yellow WSHP logo strewn across the body probably wouldn't be a car thief's first choice.

"Robbie Coates is back."

"How do you know?"

"That's his car." Midge waved in the direction of a two-tone lime green and orange vintage Volkswagen Beetle. It was sitting next to Hackett's bright red Lexus convertible, still parked where he'd left it on the last night of his life.

"And it looks like he knows."

"Probably. But how can you be sure?"

"That's Duckheimer's car." Midge pointed to a tan Taurus. "I definitely don't need to be here for this." Midge jolted into reverse and dashed out of the lot and headed down to Pleasant Street. "Just as well he hears it from Duckheimer."

"Maybe he already heard," Eliza said, again working the imaginary emergency brake as Midge shot by a creeping black Escalade in the no passing lane. "I mean he's pretty close to Ashley. Maybe she called him."

"Maybe. But either way, I'm glad I don't have to break the news. He's a pretty good kid considering his family's so screwed up. And for some reason he idolized Hackett."

"Guess he was some sort of father figure."

"Yeah, and believe it or not, Hackett was an improvement over the real one.

"Oh, God. That's not saying much."

"Well, Dan Coates was a big time bastard. Very abusive. Used to scream at his wife in the middle of the A&P, at the PTA, wherever. Called her some horrible names. Even made me blush a few times."

"That bad, huh?" Eliza let out an uncomfortable laugh. "Did he hit her, too?"

"Probably. I only saw her with a black eye once. She swore she ran into a door, the usual routine. Robbie said he never saw him raise his fist. Robbie says 'the Beast' as he calls him, was too remote to get physical with them. But he was always cursing them out, the wife and Robbie and his little sister who was asthmatic or something, I think. Very sickly."

"His mom lives up in Rhinebeck now, right?"

"Yeah, she moved there after the divorce. Moved back with the kids to be near her parents. I think Robbie was about fifteen at the time. Ethan would know. He was two or three years behind him in school."

"Where did the father go?"

"Stayed here for a while. Worked over there at Oscar Oleo's as a mechanic." Midge drove by the old garage, gave Oscar a little honk.

"Oh, that must have been interesting," Eliza smiled and waved as Oscar looked up and waved them off dismissively.

"It was. From what I heard, he turned his anger on Oscar one day and that was that."

"What do you mean?"

"He just took off. Don't think anyone's heard from him since."

"Not even Robbie?" Eliza thought fleetingly of her own limited relationship with her elusive father. Earnest Chase had been her mother's third husband. A hard-luck actor turned insurance salesman, he moved to New Hampshire after the divorce when Eliza was six, a few years before she landed the *Family Dancing* gig. He remarried an English professor, and while Eliza had only seen him every other summer and occasional holidays, at least she always knew where he was.

"I don't think Robbie cares, but it is sad."

"I hear his mom is sick."

"Very. Sounds like there's not much time left."

"What a shame."

"Yeah, and he had so much invested in Hackett. Emotionally."

"Well, sounds like a clear case of transference."

"Maybe so, Dr. Sylvan."

"Don't start with me, okay." Eliza laughed. "But maybe he wasn't such a bad guy. I mean he took Robbie under his wing. And Ashley, too."

"Yeah, well I think she was hoping to find herself under something other than his wing." Midge snorted, zipped by a sparsely attended tag sale on Orchid Avenue. "In the middle of nowhere on the emptiest of weekends, what do they expect?"

"Miriam Sussman came." Eliza laughed, pointing to the retired librarian milling cheerfully through a cloister of knick knacks.

"God, that geezer can always be found at the scene of the crime," Midge said, shaking her head and flooring the gas pedal.

"Speaking of which, "Eliza said, grabbing the glove compartment for leverage, and working the imaginary brake. "You can't seriously think Ashley killed Hackett."

"I don't know. But I've had enough angry girl drama for one day."

"Don't worry. Hannah will come around."

"If she does she does. In the meantime, let her hang out with that walking Halloween costume for all I care."

"Yeah, that guy was a little strange."

"Probably a theatre person. Up your alley." Midge laughed as they hit Pleasant Street. "Anyway, Gus will be back tomorrow. So he can deal with her nonsense for a change." Midge negotiated the Volvo around the crowded little lot behind Soup Opera. "Here you are, Your Majesty, and once again, in one piece."

"Much obliged." Eliza slid out of the car. "Now go home, relax."

"I will, indeed. Think I'll soak in the Jacuzzi until I prune."

"Well, maybe you'll soak up a clue or two while you're at it."

"And maybe you'll stir up a few. Either way we'll call each other first," Midge called out the window as Eliza headed to Soup Opera's back entrance.

Eliza laughed, turned around "Who'd you think I'd call? Duckheimer?"

Midge shook her head. "If that's the first name to pop into your head, maybe old Sunny Sylvan is on to something." Midge chuckled as she high-tailed it out of the parking lot. "I hate to admit it, but maybe the old fraud really does know her stuff."

Chapter 10

Eliza and Tom spent Saturday dinner in the comfort of an unspoken détente. She didn't press for details and he didn't admonish her to stay out of the Hackett case. They ate take-out garlic shrimp and house lo mein from Lucky Pearl in the dining nook in the kitchen of the Gordon Family Museum.

After feeding him a spring roll form her chopsticks, Eliza scooted to his side of the nook, nestled her cheek against his.

"Do you think this is a good idea?" Tom smiled; a light blush dotted his cheeks, accentuating his cute Kirk Douglas dimples. "I mean someone could walk in on us."

"Like who?" Eliza kissed Tom, a passionate garlic and ginger scented dance between her lips and his. "The nearest neighbor is a mile away. But all that's gonna change. Pretty soon we may actually see people walk by the window. Voyeurs. What fun." Eliza laughed, kissed Tom again.

"I was thinking Jonas could burst in," Tom said, pulling away. "That could be kind of awkward. I mean he is Eddie's brother."

"I don't think he'd care," Eliza said, fishing for water chestnuts and peppers in the shrimp dish. "Anyway, haven't you heard? The international man of mystery left town."

"No. Where'd he go?"

"He said he had an emergency meeting in Washington, D.C. Left last night."

"Wonder what that's about? On the weekend, too."

"Probably got summoned by the White House."

"Nothing would surprise me."

"I still don't get him. I wish someone would fill me in."

"What can I tell you? Eddie's little brother was always an enigma."

"Tell me about it. He's been living here what? Three, no four months, and I still don't know why he came back or what he's up to."

"Well, if anyone can solve the mystery." Tom laughed, fed Eliza a crisp water chestnut from his chopsticks.

"Don't worry I'm working on it."

"As long as that's all you're working on."

"Yes, sir." Eliza bristled, but decided not to let a passing comment ruin the evening.

After loading the dishes into the dishwasher to Ella Fitzgerald's jazzy serenade, Eliza and Tom went outside and strolled the palatial well-manicured grounds. The looming elms and oaks provided a sheltering summer evening shade.

"Think you'll miss this?" Tom asked as they ventured near the pool.

"Yes and no...mostly no, I think." Eliza was finally ready to leave, to move on to the next phase of her life. *I am; I really am,* she thought as she gazed into Tom's kind face aglow in the shimmering reflection of the pool's cool water.

"It will be good for you," Tom said, guiding his fingers through her long honey hair. "The move."

Eliza nodded but the tranquility was abruptly interrupted by a succession of shrill car horn honks and Lou Bracco's gruff, gravel-tinged rebuke.

"Those damn kids again!" Lou shrieked.

"Him, I'll miss," Eliza said with a chuckle as she and Tom walked towards the entrance gate to confront the commotion. Lou Bracco, the caretaker of the Gordon estate for over thirty years, was already lambasting a scrawny kid with an acne and stubble dotted face.

"Turn that crap off!" Lou said, waving a battered badminton racket. A short, compact man, who'd enjoyed a less than illustrious stint as a minor league shortstop, Lou, now in his mid sixties, continued a military-style exercise regimen that kept him in tip-top shape.

The car horns had been exchanged for a pulsating blast of Simon & Garfunkel's' "The Sounds of Silence."

"I don't see the point, but I do get the irony," Eliza said, hanging back a bit as Tom approached Lou and the teen.

"What's the problem here?" Tom stood tall, tightened his abs, transforming his navy polo shirt and tan khakis into a police uniform just by the way he walked. "Son, you're on private property." He looked the kid in the eye. "And you'll have to turn that music off."

"It's a free country, isn't it?" The kid said, rocking back and forth in a pair of tattered sneakers. That motion reminded Eliza of someone, but she couldn't think of whom.

"Yes, but citizenship comes with certain responsibilities. And one of them is to be a thoughtful member of the community. And that noise level violates local ordinances. You could be fined."

"What are you gonna do? Call the cops?"

"I don't have to," Tom said, whipping out his badge. "I am the Goodship Police Chief."

The music instantly evaporated, leaving behind a jarring silence. "Just get in the car, Nero," the driver said. "Are you arresting us?"

"Let me see your license, please," Tom said, his head leaning into the driver's side window." Tom was already jotting down the license plate number. He flipped open his cell and called in the plate and the driver's name."

Eliza walked closer, stood right behind Tom and Lou. The driver looked familiar. She recognized him. The spiky blue-black punk hair, the kabuki white skin, the dramatic black eye-liner. He was that odd guy she and Midge had seen watering the plants at the Nature Center earlier.

Within a few minutes, Tom was wrapping up his call "Okay, thanks."

"You arresting us?" The kabuki guy asked.

"No, I'll let you go with a warning. But show some respect, Mr. Whelan." Tom handed the freaky guy his license and registration.

The driver nodded. "Okay. Just tell 'em: 'The Quiet is here and we're making noise. And no one can stop it!'" the driver tossed a flyer out the window. He'd been so quiet at the Nature Center. Now he was calling himself—or some group he was a part of—*The Quiet*—and making an awful lot of noise about it.

The white van sped away.

"Why'd you let him go?" Lou asked, now waving the racket at Tom.

"They're just joy-riding. Nothing to worry about."

"That's what you think," Lou groused as he walked back up the long drive. "That's why you can't solve a murder around here. Too soft."

In the distance "The Sounds of Silence" was blaring again.

"What'd I tell ya?" Lou laughed, handed Eliza the flyer.

"What's it say?" Tom asked.

Eliza read the flyer aloud: "The Quiet. Hear it. Know it. Be it. Labor Day Weekend the world will finally listen."

"Can't wait," Lou said with a dismissive wave as he headed towards the caretaker's cottage. "Night, folks."

"Night, Lou. Thanks," Eliza said.

"Want to call it into *The Grapevine?*" Tom laughed, offering his cell phone to Eliza.

"I'll pass," she said as they walked back to the house. "What do you make of it?

"I don't know. It's probably just kid stuff."

"That guy—the driver—he works at the Nature Center. Midge and I saw him this morning when we visited Hannah."

"Uh oh."

"What?"

"Nothing. But if you're gonna call Midge can it wait until tomorrow? I don't want to spend the whole night babysitting two yenta-sleuths."

"Yenta-sleuths? Nice description." Eliza smiled. "We can get cards printed up."

"So can it wait?"

"Sure. I've got nothing to report." *Not really,* Eliza thought. *Nothing that I understand anyway.*

"You called in the plate. Who's it registered to?"

"That ma'am is official police business." Tom laughed. "But since he was being annoying on your property, I guess it's okay. The plate came up clean, the driver too. Registered to a Carl Whelan, 28 years old, no traffic violations, no criminal convictions, no cases pending. He's a veritable boy scout."

"A kabuki boy scout." Eliza and Tom laughed as they walked arm in arm up the long cobblestone walkway.

*****

Back at the house, Eliza and Tom put the weird nonsense behind them and relaxed, curled up on her bed and slipped in a DVD. While Hitchcock and Tallulah hissed at each other, Tom and Eliza watched *Marley and Me*. Eliza wondered how her felines would manage in the new, smaller quarters. Of course, for two years before moving into the museum, they had navigated each other in her tiny Astor Place apartment in New York City.

The comedy about a mischievous family dog turned into a sentimental tearjerker. Neither Eliza nor Tom tried to conceal their tears from each other. A good sign, Eliza thought. Especially for Tom. Of course, Eliza had seen Tom cry in front of her before, once when they were remembering Eddie. And two or three times in a movie theatre. And he shared a good cry last fall when she and Midge had found themselves in a dangerous situation in a motel room with a murderer. She had promised him then that she'd ditch the "Cagney and Lacy business," as he'd called it. So she realized when Tom scoffed at her sleuthing that he wasn't just being Ricky Ricardo to her Lucy. He was worried about her. She understood that. But still, something about the Hackett case got her hooked. And this Quiet business got her intrigued, too. So there was no turning back. She'd just have to be careful. And discreet.

When the movie was over, Eliza brought up bowls of pistachio ice cream and fortune cookies. They switched to the TV, waiting to catch the late news, half-watching the back end of an old *Law & Order*.

"Good ice cream," Tom said, lapping up the treat as Hitchcock pounced on the bed.

"Don't even think about it." Eliza shook her head as she cuddled the fat cat. Normally she'd give in and give him a little in a dish, but the dreaded vet visit was coming up and she was already worried he'd tip the scales.

Tom polished off his last spoonful. "Delicious." He turned to Eliza, pulled her in for a kiss. "Even more delicious."

"You sweet talking me, Chief?"

"Doing my best."

While they smooched, Hitchcock found his way to Eliza's abandoned ice cream. He slipped his little head into the bowl, working his ambitious tongue around the melting mound.

Eliza had her head nestled against Tom's chest when she spied the culprit. "Hitchcock!" Eliza shrieked as she bolted off the bed and grabbed the now nearly empty bowl. "Great! Now I'll never hear the end of it." Hitchcock sauntered away. Tom laughed, stretched out his arms, inviting Eliza back to bed.

On TV, a twitchy suspect insisted he couldn't have killed the victim. "I was with my woman. All night. Go ask her."

"Guess you're my alibi," Tom said.

"Do you need one?" Eliza slipped in next to Tom and playfully rubbed his shoulders.

"You never know," Tom said, smiling, enjoying his massage. "Victoria Salinger claimed she was watching a movie with her aunt up in Ridgefield the night Hackett was killed. That's her alibi."

"Well, it's got to be at least an hour's drive."

"Yeah, but the aunt's up in her eighties. She told Duckheimer she fell asleep."

"So you think she had time to drive to the station, kill Hackett and drive back without the aunt ever missing her?" Tom's shrug interfered with the rhythm of the massage. "Sit still."

"The aunt says she didn't wake up until seven thirty Thursday morning. By then Victoria was in the kitchen scrambling eggs and watching *The Today Show.*

You buying it?"

"I don't know. But Duckheimer thinks she's our girl. Her initials on the studio window…in lipstick…seems to have sealed her fate. With him anyway."

"What about you, Chief?"

"I'm not so sure."

"Me neither," Eliza whispered. "Too obvious, right?"

"Never underestimate the obvious suspects. But…well, it's got to make sense. And…"

"She doesn't?"

"I just don't know why she'd write her initials. She doesn't strike me as a whack job or someone who wants to get caught. And, what's her motive? He owed her back alimony. But if she killed him, she wouldn't collect."

"Plus he had that new gig. He would start making more money."

"A lot more." Tom shook his head. "Think Duckheimer's got to go back to the drawing board."

"He better watch his back. You'll probably solve it first."

"It's not a competition," Tom said, sitting up, facing Eliza. "It's a team effort."

"Of course." Eliza didn't mention Midge's revelation about Ashley's lipstick. Ashley seemed like a far-fetched suspect and Eliza didn't want to be the one to point a finger at an innocent person. She also didn't want Tom to know she was actually on the team, *working* on the case. He knew, of course, but she didn't want to say it aloud.

"Oh, you forgot your fortune," Eliza said, tossing Tom a fortune cookie. "Open it."

Tom cracked open the tasteless little cookie; Eliza opened hers too. "Cute."

"What's it say?"

"If you're hungry eat more Chinese food." They laughed. "How 'bout yours?"

"Listen to your intuition. It will show you all the answers you need." Eliza beamed, slipped her lips against Tom's cheek.

"And just what does your intuition tell you now?"

"It tells me to stop asking so many questions."

"A smart girl, your intuition. Very smart." Tom pulled Eliza close.

No more questions. Not tonight, Eliza thought. Tom caressed Eliza's neck.

"I'm still hungry," Tom said, stroking Eliza's luscious hair, kissing her sensual lips. "But not for Chinese food."

They snuggled, settling in for a cozy night. On the very bed Dr. Sylvan had wanted her to ditch.

Chapter 11

Sunday was a different story. A muggy, miserable day, Tom and Eliza went into New York City to catch a matinee and an early dinner with Eliza's friend Maddie and her husband Kevin. Tom didn't like the play, a rambling off-off Broadway affair called *I Love You, Richard Nixon,* about a woman who falls into a coma in the middle of Watergate and wakes up halfway through the Carter administration and spends the show writing love letters and stalking the ex-president. He also didn't like all the fawning attention the director, Stanley Ranier, an old pal from her soap opera days, showered upon Eliza—the way the guy gently stroked her shimmering mauve and brown print sundress. It didn't seem to matter that Stanley's boyfriend was the costume designer.

Dinner was no better. They wound up in SoHo at a little vegan joint owned by Maddie's sister-in-law. Between the stuffed acorn squash and tofu and veggie kabobs, Tom endured a non-stop skewering from Maddie's husband, who even Eliza had to admit was a loud lout with few visibly virtuous qualities. The guy—who worked the floor of the stock exchange during the week and harbored movie producing aspirations—reminded Eliza of Hackett. He didn't look like the slain big mouth. No, Kevin was a tall bean pole with a thick head of sandy hair, but his cocky attitude and that horrific print shirt, blue spilling into red and green, a talentless child's finger painting mess oozed Hackett's sleazy spirit. And he kept calling Tom "Sheriff Taylor," as in *The Andy Griffith Show*. It could have been worse; he could have called him "Barney Fife." Maddie didn't help either. She kept pressing Tom for details on the Hackett case. Eliza wasn't sure how she'd even heard of it; Tom glared at Eliza, of course, sure she'd flapped her yenta lips. But she hadn't said a word. Turns out, the story had made its way onto Page Six of *The New York Post*. Eliza didn't get the big city gossip appeal. After all, Hackett had yet to take his brash bite out of the Big Apple. She figured someone at the tabloid either lived in Goodship or read *The Grapevine*.

"He really can't talk about an on-going investigation," Eliza finally said, after Tom's third or fourth polite rebuff eluded the suddenly obtuse host. Eliza shot Maddie *the* look, that dagger-sharp look, with the right eyebrow arched in disdain that they'd given each other for years, since their early days working on the sit-com *Family Dancing*, when they had played mischievous junior high pals and created it as a mock tribute to their tight-assed tutor, Ruth. Eliza knew the gesture would finally shut Maddie up. And it did. But the damage had already been done.

By the time they were on the train going back to Goodship, Tom was barely grunting monosyllabic responses to Eliza's awkward attempts to get a conversation going. "Don't think it's headed to Broadway," Eliza said as a herd of rowdy teens, laughing and carousing trudged by. "The play, *I Love You, Richard Nixon*, I mean."

"No," Tom grunted. "Guess not."

Another two teens trampled by shouting "Losers!" as they caught up to their pals.

"Guess the nap's out." Eliza smiled. The air-conditioning was, too. She fanned herself with her Playbill.

"Yep." Tom shifted in his seat.

Between New Rochelle and Larchmont, a few of the kids started snapping each other's photos with camera phones. "Make that ape face. I'm gonna send it to Chloe and all her prissy Facebook friends."

"Oh, there's a real useful invention," Tom snorted.

"Bet you'd like it if someone took a picture of the murder." Eliza smiled, playfully hit his khaki covered knee.

"Show me that and we'll talk." Tom cracked a little, showing the faintest hint of that sweet Santini smile as they stopped at the Mamaroneck station. A few stops later, as they pulled into Goodship, he was ready for a frozen yogurt cone and a passionate goodnight kiss.

*****

With a busy Monday looming, Tom dropped Eliza off by nine. Hitchcock eagerly greeted her in the majestic foyer, his fat black tail glistening like silk in the subdued light of the chandelier. He rubbed his plump body against her legs, purring impatiently. She picked him up, cradled his opulence. "Did you really miss me that much? Or do you have an ulterior motive?" She smiled, shaking her head as they crossed over the marbled threshold of the kitchen. The cat dashed out of her clutches and bounded towards the big cat dish in the corner.

"It was full when I left." Eliza was surprised to find Tallulah languidly stretching next to the now empty dish. "Not buying it," Eliza said. She'd purposely left them a double portion, enough to satisfy both their morning and evening appetites. Still, guilt got the better of her and she reflexively filled the dish with dry Fancy Feast bits. She also refreshed the water bowl. "But that's it 'til morning," she said, as she deposited the snack. She didn't believe for a single second that Tallulah had polished off her own meager portion, let alone Hitchcock's substantial share.

"Obvious suspects," she chuckled as she grabbed a small bottle of Poland Spring lemon and lime and headed up the long, winding staircase. "Don't dismiss anyone. But they have to make sense."

As Eliza washed away the summer in the city grime in a soothing shower, she found herself incessantly humming David Bowie's "Young Americans." Couldn't get it out of her head. It was that one line referring to President Nixon that had ensnared her attention and wouldn't let it go.

That silly, awful little play, she thought as she ambled into the bedroom, *The New York Times Magazine* in one hand, Arbuckle, the big teddy bear Eddie had bought her in the early days of their whirlwind courtship, in the other. She plopped on the bed, ready to unwind. *So it wasn't the greatest day, so what?* It wasn't so bad. At least the ending had been better than the beginning. She and Tom were still okay. *Another good sign,* she thought. Anyone could have a good time when everything was running smoothly. But to still like each other after a crappy day, that really said something positive about the relationship. And that chocolate-minty coated kiss wasn't a bad way to wrap up the weekend either.

"Hackett!" Eliza bolted upright; sat against the headboard, still clutching Arbuckle. She was suddenly replaying the conversation Bert and Oscar had had the other day about the loudmouth, how he hated all the presidents. Except Nixon. *He dug us into China...and he liked to tape every conversation.*

How could this tidbit help her figure out who had killed Hackett?

An important connection was coming to her, she could feel it forming, breaking through the cluttered cobwebs of thoughts, Monday's menu specials, to-do lists for the move, etc. But before it could make its way to the front of the line, the phone rang. It was Midge checking in for the weekend recap.

"The play was no great shakes. And to tell the truth, neither was dinner," Eliza said, responding to Midge's inquiry. "How was your day?"

"Nothing from nothing."

"I thought Gus was coming home today."

"Oh, yeah. He was the first nothing."

Eliza laughed. "So how was the Chicago Food Fest?"

"He said it was okay. I'm sure he ate like a pig. But he doesn't look like he gained an ounce."

"Doesn't seem fair."

"It's not. Oh, wait, but he did come back with some interesting news....sad really and strange. Very strange."

"What happened?"

"While he was there, he heard someone shot some controversial cable TV host right outside the studio."

"Wow. Did he die?"

"Yeah, *she* did."

"Guess being a big mouth is an equal opportunity profession. With equal occupational hazards."

"Yeah, "Midge said. "And it's weird, right? I mean right after Hackett."

"Yeah...but you don't think there's a connection, do you?"

"No. I mean how could there be?"

"It's a pretty creepy coincidence, though," Eliza said, rubbing Arbuckle's plush plump tummy.

"God, these people. Their mouths can really kill them. Glad I'm just a DJ."

"I wouldn't say 'just.'"

"I'm not fishing for compliments this late on a Sunday night." Midge laughed. "Do you think Tom and Duckheimer will make an arrest soon?"

"Actually, I hope not. I think they're on the wrong track."

"So I guess we'll have to get on it."

"Think we already are."

Midge wrapped up the call, promising to stop by Soup Opera after her show for a brainstorming session.

Eliza got back into bed, closed her eyes, letting the tinny piano music of a Lillian Gish silent movie lull her to sleep. Images of the kids on the train, clicking their camera phones flashing through her mind.

Chapter 12

"You better nab that snake behind the ghastly *Grapevine* or you'll have another murder to solve." Lois Danziger—all four feet-eight inches of her—was vigorously waving her cell phone as she cornered Chief Tom Santini and Detective Fred Duckheimer in a no longer inconspicuous back booth at Soup Opera. It was after two on Monday afternoon and the already sparse late summer crowd had pretty much petered out. The few remaining folks—at the counter or scattered about in tables and booths—were now riveted to this latest melodrama.

"May I suggest you put that away before Chief Santini here has to haul you in for possession of a deadly weapon," Detective Duckheimer said, flinching, reacting to the uncomfortable proximity Lois' very animated cell phone had to his ham and Swiss wrap, not to mention his head.

"Have you seen it today?" Lois ignored Duckheimer's warning and was still flipping the phone. The entire hullabaloo was over a photo that had popped up on *The Goodship Grapevine* earlier that morning; a rather unflattering photo of Lois dashing down Pleasant Street draped in a Sheer Genius smock, her hair tucked under a cellophane cap.

"Don't worry, Lois," Tom said, smiling as he reached his large sturdy hand out to disarm her. "No one really cares about *The Grapevine*. And anyway, most people are out of town." Tom nodded his head, signaling the many empty tables. He quickly secured the weapon, jailing the phone behind the napkin dispenser.

"It's defamation! I should sue!" Lois shrieked. "I will sue once I find out that scoundrel behind this site."

"What's all the commotion?" Eliza just popped out of the kitchen where she had stashed vats of uneaten cream of asparagus, five bean and Manhattan clam chowder into the fridge.

"My mother," Dee Dee said, leaning against the counter, her arms akimbo, revealing only slivers of tie-dyed pink and orange. She rolled her eyes, which Eliza noticed were dramatically outlined in heavy blue-black mascara, reminiscent of that odd kid at the Nature Center, whose name she learned last Saturday was Carl Whelan. "Always making a scene."

"Well, you can't really blame her," Eliza said. She'd seen the photo and figured there'd be fall-out.

"Who told her to go parading around in that get-up?" Miriam Sussman said. She had been perched at the counter, nursing a bottomless lemonade and a smoked turkey wrap for the last two hours.

"You think I'd be traipsing around like that if I didn't have to feed the damned parking meter?" Lois said, now lurching back towards the counter. "If they didn't install those freaking things I would never be in this predicament." Lois dashed back to the police booth and waved her finger at Tom.

"Hey, don't look at me," Tom said, tossing his head back to deflect Lois' menacing advances. "I don't make the law, ma'am; I just enforce it."

"C.Y.A. That's all anyone knows around here." Lois' face was now flushed a deep pink to match her snug, ill-fitting t-shirt. "Just tell me: would it kill people to do something, just one nice thing for me once in a while."

"It might," Dee Dee said with another eye roll. She shared a snicker with Miriam and Poppy Sumner, who was sitting alone at the opposite end of the counter, nibbling delicately on a grilled veggie flatbread. Poppy slid off her stool and walked over to Lois. "Here you go," she said, offering Lois her pickle wedge. Poppy's tall, slim silhouette juxtaposed with the petite waif conjured an odd, almost cartoonish symmetry.

"What's this?" Lois clutched the soggy pickle.

"Just trying to be nice." Poppy smiled as she headed back to her stool.

"Guess she was out of sour grapes," Miriam snickered.

"Hilarious!" Lois hurled the pickle across the counter.

"Whoa!" Eliza ducked as the flying condiment flew by her head, hitting Harpo Marx on the *Duck Soup* poster before making a soggy landing on the floor.

"Wow, Lois you got a great arm. The Mets could use you," Dee Dee said.

"That's Mother to you. Don't forget I'm still funding your smart mouth, missy."

"Oh you're a mother alright." Dee Dee's eye roll was quickly quashed by Lois' pathetic pout. "Sorry Mom. Really. But don't make it such a big deal. It's sort of a funky photo."

Eliza shot Dee Dee an incredulous look. "Not exactly helping," she whispered. "Look, Lois, I know you're upset. But really if they had to run it, this was a good week. Most folks are away."

"I'm still suing."

"Who can you sue?" Miriam asked.

"Oh I'll sue. When I find out that sleaze hustler, their ass is grass."

"I know you are but what am I?" Poppy laughed.

"Keep it up, "Lois said. "And you'll all be sorry."

"I wouldn't start threatening people, Mom. Not with the police within earshot." Dee Dee stuck a lemon wedge in her mouth to quell an unwelcome outburst of laughter.

"Don't think it would hold up." Miriam shook her head, her gray Brillo pad do barely moving. "It's not libel if it's true, even if it is unflattering. And it is you in that photo, right?"

"Yes, but I never agreed to have my picture taken. And I certainly never gave any approval for that site to run it."

"It's a murky area, I'm afraid, Mrs. Danzinger," Detective Duckheimer said, flinching as he approached Lois near the register. "The law hasn't exactly caught up with technology. There are few laws protecting people from others' publishing photos over the Internet."

"Even without the person's approval?"

"I'm afraid so."

"And if you're a public person or celebrity you have even fewer rights in this area," Tom said, standing next to Duckheimer.

"Public person?" Lois scoffed. "I'm a private citizen. *Very* private."

"Not really. You do have a public persona," Tom said, winking at Eliza, as he settled his tab. "Face it, Lois, in Goodship you are a celebrity. Everyone knows you."

"Well. I do run the area's premier hotel." Lois now stood tall (as tall as she could), holding her white–blonde curly coiffed head prouder.

"Still, if you contact the site and they're on the up and up, they should do the right thing and take it down," Tom said. "Have you tried that?"

"No, but I will." Lois offered an ambivalent smile as she held out her hand. "My phone, Chief?"

"Promise to behave yourself?"

"Yes."

Tom handed her the cell phone.

"Fame has its price," Poppy said, her ebullient expression erased, replaced by a sunken dour visage that accentuated every one of her forty-six years

"I suppose it does," Lois said, now beaming as she walked to the exit. "But I still expect you to nab that snake, Chief."

"I'm on it," Tom laughed.

As Lois slipped out the door, Jonas pushed through, a harried expression on his perfectly chiseled face, a black leather laptop bag slung over his shoulder.

"Ah, the prodigal returns," Eliza said, handing Tom his change. Jonas, Eliza noticed, looked more wilted than she'd ever seen him; he was wearing a wrinkled light green Oxford shirt and a pair of tan slacks that looked like he may have worn them—and then slept in them—all weekend. He also sported a few days' worth of stubble, something only extremely good-looking young men could pull off. He was one such fortunate creature.

"I have indeed." Jonas waved, offered a wan smile.

Eliza sighed as she wiped down the counter. Jonas was a very handsome man; there was no getting around that. And he did remind Eliza of Eddie. But as she glanced up at Tom, handsome too and so strong in his uniform, she realized she was indeed smitten with the Goodship Police Chief. Suddenly, she couldn't wait to move out of the Museum and into *her* new Briar Ridge townhouse. Dr. Sylvan should be quite pleased.

"I need to speak with you," Jonas said, tapping Tom on the shoulder. "Both of you." He nodded at Duckheimer as the two cops loitered in the entry alcove.

"Go ahead, Mr. Gordon," Duckheimer said, stroking his bushy mustache with a small calico-colored brush. "Start talking."

"Not here," Jonas said, eyeing the door just as Midge charged through, chimes clanking to signal her arrival.

"Why don't we go back to the station," Tom said. "We were headed there anyway." He smiled, noting Eliza's disappointed expression, with an air kiss and a chuckle.

"Bye," Eliza said with a wave. "Don't let the door hit you on the way out," she muttered under her breath. *Talk about anti-climatic.*

The three men exited in a comical slapstick tag-team that nearly knocked Midge over.

"Was it something I said?" Midge laughed as she grabbed a stool next to Miriam.

"No, something Jonas was *about* to say." Eliza shrugged and handed Midge a Diet Pepsi bottle. "You didn't miss anything."

"Except Lois' theatrics," Dee Dee said, stashing the sugar packets under the counter.

"Except that." Eliza laughed.

"I got to get out of here." Poppy abruptly slid off her stool and darted to the door like a feral cat who'd suddenly realized she was trapped in a cage.

"What do you make of that?" Eliza asked.

"Dunno. Hope she paid you, though." Midge shook her head; the humid weather was continuing to do all sorts of interesting things to her hair. She pulled out a mirror from her satchel. "God, anyone casting an *Annie* remake? I could make it into *The Guinness Book of World Records* as the oldest Annie in history."

Eliza laughed. "We're all a little weathered," she said, running her fingers through her own hair, which, while not nearly as frizzed as Midge's was not exactly enjoying a good day either.

"I'm not paying for a millionaire's wife who still has an overdue copy of *Anna Karenina*," Miriam said as she walked to the register. "And I don't tip for counter service." She handed Eliza exact change for her sandwich and lemonade. She scurried out of Soup Opera, her big straw tote, brimming with at least one shelf's worth of books, weighing heavily on her right shoulder.

"Millionaire's wife huh?" Midge laughed. "Glad someone has access to Alex's bank account. Don't worry, I'll cover Poppy's tab."

"No need," Eliza said, waving a twenty dollar bill she found stowed under Poppy's plate.

They may have been no closer to solving the Hackett murder and business was slow. But with so many suspects overpaying their lunch checks, Eliza was turning a profit anyway.

Chapter 13

"Maybe she really was in love with him." Midge tossed a bag of mixed field greens into a large wooden salad bowl. It was after six and Gus and Nicky would be traipsing in soon expecting dinner. Tonight, they'd be disappointed; salad and leftover BBQ chicken would almost certainly fetch a cacophonous stereophonic groan. But it was too hot, and Midge was too scattered to care.

"You still think Poppy had a thing for Hackett?" Eliza, pressed into duty, was slicing cucumbers and tomatoes along Midge's butcher block counter, earning her keep for the family supper she was about to share.

Midge shrugged, grabbed a garlic clove from the net above the sink. "Alex is pretty convinced," she said, smashing the garlic against a board. "He told me she would always go on and on about how special he was. She invited him to dinner every other week. God, can you imagine?"

"No," Eliza laughed, tossed the cukes into Midge's salad bowl. "So she was taken with him, so what? A lot of people are taken with celebrities and people with charisma. It doesn't mean there was anything romantic going on."

"Maybe. So tell me why she's been sleeping in the guest room since the murder?" Midge added olive oil, dried mustard and red wine vinegar into a small green

Fiesta bowl that already contained smashed bits of garlic.

"She's been in the guest room *since* the murder, not before?" Eliza plated the tomato slices, along with rings of purple onion on a green Fiesta serving dish.

"What's your point?"

"Well, wouldn't it make more sense—if she had really been involved with Hackett—for her to move out while he was still alive?"

"I guess. But why has she been acting so strange?" Midge stuck a lettuce leaf into the dressing, took a bite. "Needs something." She shrugged, doused a leaf and handed it to Eliza to try.

"Pepper. A pinch of salt," Eliza said. "Just a pinch."

"I know; you can always add, but you can't subtract." Midge added pepper and a gentle sprinkling of kosher salt into her salad elixir.

"What was that about at Soup Opera today?" Eliza tasted another leaf Midge had slipped into her mouth. "Perfecto," she nodded.

"That's what I mean," Midge said, working a knife around a loaf of Italian bread with Paul Bunyan's gentle touch. Eliza, realizing her pal was getting worked up over this Poppy business, subtly disarmed Midge and finished slicing the bread.

After surrendering peaceably, Midge went about setting out butter and olives on the table. "She's been acting so daffy lately. Alex says she plays tapes of Hackett's shows over and over. Every night, locked in the guest room."

"She taped them?"

"Either that or she got Alex to make her copies".

"You tape all the shows, right?"

"Well, all the talk shows, public affairs shows and specials. We only keep tapes of guest interviews for the rest of the day."

"So Tom and Duckheimer must have heard Hackett's shows?"

"Yeah, I guess. The last one anyway. And any others they wanted. I know Alex gave them access to the whole archive."

"Maybe there was some wacko caller who had it in for Hackett."

"Take a number," Midge laughed, put out pitchers of sun-seeped iced tea and Newman's Own low-cal lemonade. "I mean who didn't have it in for him?"

"Well, Robbie and Ashley." Eliza bit her tongue; she'd almost forgotten about Ashley's lipstick on the studio window.

"That's another one who's been acting awfully jumpy. That Ashley really had a thing for Hackett. God, I almost suggested she go see Dr. Sylvan the other day. Found her blubbering in the bathroom. And get this: she was wearing one of his hideous Hawaiian print shirts. Looked like a muumuu on her."

"So you're over Ashley as a suspect?"

"Who knows? But just because it was her lipstick shade, doesn't mean anything. Anyone could get that shade. Maybe the ex-wife uses it."

"Or someone could have found a stick at the station. Maybe she left it behind. Or maybe someone was trying to frame her." Eliza was so excited; she was waving a cucumber slice around.

"No playing with your food until everyone gets here." Midge laughed, as the cucumber slice flew out of Eliza's hand, landing on the butcher block counter next to the kitschy Betty Boop napkin dispenser. "Nice arm."

"Sorry, I'm turning into Lois Danziger." Eliza laughed. "You know Bert Santini said Hackett had this thing, almost an obsession with Richard Nixon. He collected all sorts of books and memorabilia."

"So he had a thing for Tricky Dickie, so?"

"So, I don't know. But Nixon had a thing about taping every conversation."

"Yeah, I remember that's how the whole Watergate mess blew up in his face. So what's ancient history got to do with Hackett?"

"Nothing. Except...I don't know, maybe Hackett had a thing about taping, too."

"Sit down and start eating," Midge said, putting out light green Fiesta plates and darker green salad bowls. "Your blood sugar must be low; I just told you he taped all his shows."

"I know, but maybe he...I mean, could he also have taped regular conversations, I mean off-the-air?"

"You mean you think he bugged the station?"

"I don't know," Eliza said, sitting down in one of the stiff Federalist style kitchen table chairs, soaking up all the comfort of an old church pew. "Is it possible?"

"I don't know. I guess." Midge shrugged, headed to the doorway. "On the table, Mable!" she screamed out the door, her smooth voice echoing up the stairs and boomeranging back in the cavernous acoustics of the old Victorian. "Can't wait to see Alex's face when I tell him we have to sweep for bugs." She sat down next to Eliza.

"Ooo...bugs! Better call the Orkin man." Her son Nicky traipsed in. His baggy bright orange and royal blue shorts were hanging like deflated pool floats on his skinny frame. Eliza also noticed the ten year old—just days back from a six week stint at sleep-away soccer camp—appeared to have shot up like a hearty weed.

"Different kind of bugs," Midge said, inspecting the boy's hands and face for visible outdoor grime. "And enough television, young man. School starts next week; might as well break the couch potato habit now."

"So lame, Mom, "Nicky said, pinching off a hunk of Italian bread. "I just got home. And anyhow, I don't watch that much TV. I'm not Hannah."

"Where is Hannah, anyway?" Eliza asked, setting out serving spoons and napkins.

"Her majesty won't be joining us tonight. She's dining with some of her friends." Midge poured herself a glass of iced tea.

"Yeah those Nature Center freaks," Nicky said, stuffing the bread into his mouth, crumbs spewing down his washed out blue METS t-shirt.

"Nicholas, please, "Midge said. "And sit down. Eat like a person." Midge ran her hand across his scrawny chest. And worked her way up to his head, tousled his shaggy auburn mane. "And this, this comes off tomorrow."

"Mom!" Nicky flinched. He flopped into a chair. "They are weirdoes," he mumbled, helped himself to a chicken breast from the Fiesta platter.

"Nicky! That's not very nice." Midge glanced at the clock, wondered what was keeping Gus.

"Come on, Mom. You know they are. That girl Debbie, she only eats broccoli and tofu. And she listens to Ani DeFranco. What's up with that?"

"Sounds like she's a good role model to me," Midge laughed, fetched bottles of Wishbone, light French and Hidden Valley Ranch for the table.

"You're forgetting your vinaigrette?" Eliza asked, ladling out a spoonful and drizzling it over her salad.

"Oh, right." Midge looked stunned. "Just offering options" she covered.

"She can't be a model. That chick doesn't even shave her legs...or her pits." Nicky laughed, worked a chicken breast around his plate with that Sumner-Delano gusto.

"Excuse me?" Midge feigned annoyance, shot Eliza a quick smirk.

"What?" Nicky asked with a pre-pubescent oblivion.

"'*That chick*?' That's not the way we refer to young women in this house."

"Out of the mouths of babes," Eliza whispered, smiled.

"Go get your father." Midge rubbed Nicky's shoulder. "Dinner is served."

Nicky rolled his eyes, slid out of his chair, trailing more crumbs as he went to the doorway. "And that guy Carl looks like something out of *Twilight*. Dad! Dinner!" he bellowed, standing in the drafty alcove between the kitchen and the hallway. His voice echoing as Midge's had moments earlier.

"I could have done that myself," Midge said.

"No you couldn't," Nicky said as he slid back into his seat. "You don't want to overwork your vocal chords." Nicky laughed, resumed working his chicken.

"Have you noticed my family is filled with comedians? Obviously you missed my performance just mere moments ago." Midge laughed, slid off her chair. "I'll fetch the gourmand myself. Dig in, we don't stand on ceremonies," she instructed Eliza as she headed to the door. "Never thought I'd be calling Gus 'Late for Dinner.' Guess there's a first time for everything," she continued as she climbed the long staircase.

"Can you believe it, she's still talking." Nicky shook his mop-topped head and laughed, as he continued devouring the chicken. Funny how much the boy's mannerisms, his sense of humor, his appetite for food and life reminded Eliza of both Midge and Gus.

"So, you met Carl at the Nature Center?" Eliza poured herself a glass of lemonade and nibbled at a slice of bread; her manners wouldn't let her comply with Midge's command to start eating in earnest.

"He's a WEIRD-O!" Nicky went in for another bread basket dive.

"You know, Nicky, I think as you get older you'll find the so-called 'weirdoes' are often the most interesting people. A lot of them may even become your best friends. At least I've found that to be true in my life," Eliza said, wondering, just for a passing second, if she'd ever get to have such a conversation with a son of her own.

Nicky shrugged, lathered buttery spread onto a slice of bread. "Guess that explains why you like my mom so much." Nicky laughed.

"Guess so." Eliza laughed, too.

"What's a vow of silence?" Nicky asked finally, raking his fork through his salad bowl.

"Try your mom's vinaigrette. I think it'll make your salad yummy," Eliza said, passing the dressing bowl to Nicky. "What makes you ask about a vow of silence?"

"I heard Hannah tell Debbie that fre…that Carl guy told her she should take one."

"Vow of silence?" Gus asked as he ambled in. *It must be genetic,* Eliza thought as she watched Gus, like a laser, dart for the bread basket before he even sat down. She also noticed how handsome and slim Gus looked in his stone white shorts and purple polo shirt. Midge had been right about Gus. That trip to the Food Fest in Chicago didn't seem to add a single ounce to his sleek, Greek God physique.

"We gained one, now we're missing another. Can't get you Delanos in one place at the same time. Where's Midge?" Eliza asked

"Freshening up," Gus laughed. "A vow of silence is not something we're acquainted with in this family," Gus said, sitting down, running his hands through his wavy black hair. He skewered a chicken breast and thigh and immediately plunged in. "Especially your mother."

"Especially your mother what?" Midge returned, resumed her seat. "Will you eat already? Before there's nothing left." She nudged Eliza as she handed her the chicken platter. "Dinner at the Delanos is every man for himself."

"Guess that means you can't eat anything. You're not a man," Nicky said, crumbs spewing ebulliently down his chin. "You're a girl. An old girl."

"Clowns to the left, jokers to the right," Midge said, glancing at Eliza as she commandeered the chicken platter. "So what were you talking about?"

"Vow of silence," Nicky repeated. "No one will tell me what it is."

Midge shook her head, puckered her lips in disdain. "Oh, no, in radio a vow of silence could be considered career suicide." Midge grabbed a leg and started working her salad.

"Could work at home, though," Gus laughed as he poured a zealous portion of the vinaigrette over his salad.

"You want silence?" Midge asked, rolling her eyes and waving a hunk of Italian bread. "I'll give you a silence you can hear into Christmas."

"What you're mother is so generously about to demonstrate is not a vow of silence, Nicky," Gus laughed, gently rubbing Midge's shoulder. "It's what's known as the silent treatment. And I'll take it any way I can get it, lady." Gus laughed.

Chapter 14

Eliza's new neighbor at #20 Briar Ridge was blasting the *West Side Story* soundtrack and frolicking through his sprinkler. Eliza smiled as she watched the man, middle-aged and chubby, dance through his artificial summer rain, clad in nothing but a snug pair of bright purple and red Madras plaid Bermuda shorts. He sang, along, off-key at a youthfully uninhibited volume.

She'd like it here, Eliza thought as she waited on *her* front lawn for the inspector to make his rounds checking the roof, foundation, plumbing, electricity, every nook and cranny of the brand new town house. She was expecting a stellar, worry-free report. And enjoying a break from the slow–go end of summer service at Soup Opera. Dee Dee and Sam could handle things. And Bert Santini said he'd stop in to check on them.

Bert's son was a different story. Tom was elusive these days, pensive and remote, the way he always got when he was entrenched in a big case. After dinner at Midge's last night, Eliza had called Tom, asking him what he made of those flyers floating around town, the ones that all summer, had commanded people to essentially "Be Quiet." She wasn't sure why it bothered her so much now, but something was rattling around in her brain after Nicky had asked about a vow of silence. In a noisy town filled with blabbermouths, Eliza wondered why there was a sudden obsession with silence. And that "Carl freak," as Nicky had called him, the odd guy at the Nature Center, who had driven by

Eliza's last weekend, tossing out one of those flyers and calling his group The Quiet, had apparently asked Nicky's sister Hannah to take a vow of silence. There had to be some connection. But what?

"The cops are behind it, right? You're afraid someone's gonna spill the beans," Eliza had said, broaching the subject with what she thought was delicacy and humor. "You can tell me. I won't tell a soul. Not even Midge or Jill Dondi."

"Stop trying to charm me into releasing classified information," Tom said without a hint of humor.

"Classified, huh? Guess I am on to something."

"This is not a game, Eliza. Goodnight." Tom abruptly ended the call.

Eliza was stung by Tom's curt cut-off, but tried to shrug it off as a hazard of his profession. And she figured she was, in fact, on to something. But what? And why should she bother with those crazy flyers when Paul Hackett's murderer remained at large.

That was none of her business either, of course, she thought, as she spun around to stare across the street where a Goodship Police car had just pulled into the driveway of #23. *Hackett's house.* Eliza was surprised to see Detective Duckheimer exit the passenger side of the vehicle, and even more shocked to see Tony Dondi––and not Tom—get out of the driver's side.

"We can see you ma'am," Tony said, rapping on the door, which still had a now dangling piece of yellow crime scene tape affixed to it. Duckheimer was peering into the big bay window.

"Ma'am, you can't be here," Tony said as a woman inside bristled by the window.

"Open the door now," Duckheimer commanded as he loudly knocked on the window.

Eliza ambled to the curb, waving to her new neighbor, who was now aiming his sprinkler in the direction of his vegetable patch, hoping to help his tomatoes and cucumbers thrive, seemingly oblivious to the police drama unfolding across the way.

"Fine. I'm out," the woman—a petite washed out blonde—said, as she walked out of the townhouse holding a big cardboard box. "What's the fuss? I was leaving anyway."

Eliza gasped as she recognized the woman. Paul Hackett's ex, Victoria Salinger. She looked even skinnier and at least ten years older than she had only a week or so ago.

"Ma'am you can't leave with…" Tony said, his arms outstretched.

"Make up your mind," Victoria huffed with an anger Eliza hadn't detected during their brief encounter at Soup Opera. *Maybe she was about to crack under the pressure,* Eliza thought.

"First you tell me I have to leave. Now you tell me I can't. Which is it, Mr. Duckhouser?" Victoria said staring at Duckheimer who was now standing by Tony Dondi's side, rocking in his infamously squeaky black rubber soled shoes. Eliza snickered. Then again, maybe Victoria wasn't ready to crack after all.

"That's *Detective Duckheimer*, Ms. Salinger. And yes, you must leave. But not with that box."

"Why? There's nothing in it that's not rightfully mine. Chief Santini said I could get my things back."

"He may have said that, but he surely meant *after* the investigation was completed," Duckheimer said as he slipped his arm around Victoria's right side, while Tony Dondi clutched her left.

Victoria, who must have felt like a sardine ready for the tin to close, didn't flinch. "I assure you, *Detective*, there is nothing in this box that will help you nab Paul's killer."

"That may be so, ma'am, but you can't really expect us to simply take your word for it," Tony said, pawing at the box's contents, holding up a tan fedora hat.

"Fine," Victoria said, surrendering the box to Tony's sturdy custody and walking down the little cobblestone path toward the driveway. "But I want every single item returned. Without any damage. All the pictures, too."

"We'll see," Duckheimer said as he and Tony closely followed her to her copper Lexus. "Now if you'll come with us, please."

"What? Why? I just gave you the box."

"Yes, ma'am, and now we have to bring you down to the station where we'll search your bag and person for any item you may have forgotten to surrender."

"My bag and *person*? You've got to be kidding me."

"No, Ms. Salinger, I'm afraid not," Duckheimer said.

"You're actually going to strip search me?"

"That particular pleasure I'll defer to a policewoman."

"This is absurd," Victoria said, her arms akimbo, her face scrunched and flushed red like a petulant child being escorted to the principal's office.

"Please, ma'am, you'll want to come voluntarily," Tony said, inching her gently toward the police car.

"Or we can arrest you," Duckheimer said, whipping out a pair of handcuffs from his back pocket. "Your choice, Ms. Salinger."

"Really, Detective," Victoria laughed. "You don't have to get so dramatic. I'll meet you there. I know the way." She headed for the driver's side of her Lexus.

"Leave the driving to us, Ms. Salinger," Duckheimer said, cajoling her into the back of the police cruiser with a jingle of the handcuffs.

"But what about my car?"

"Don't worry. We'll give you an escort later."

"Such hospitality," Victoria muttered, as she slid into the cruiser's back seat. "How did I get so lucky?"

As Duckheimer slammed the back door shut, his eyes locked with Eliza's. "Mrs. Gordon," he shook his head. "What brings you to this side of town?"

"Oh, hi, Detective," Eliza said, exuding a forced nonchalance that would get her booted off the soaps. "I'm just moving in." She pointed to her new house across the street just as the inspector, a lanky guy in white overalls, emerged waving his clipboard and flashing a no problem smile.

"What a coincidence," Duckheimer groused. "Just remember: *this* house is off-limits. It's still part of an on-going murder investigation."

"Of course, Detective," Eliza said with a smile.

"As you can see, people entering in violation of this order, do not leave of their own volition or in their own vehicle."

"Say that one three times fast," Eliza laughed.

"I'm not kidding, Mrs. Gordon. "People obstructing the investigation will be subjected to prosecution. No matter who their boyfriends may be."

"I'm just minding my own business, Detective." Eliza said, again motioning to her new house with the exaggerated gesture of a game show display girl. "I live here now."

"I'm sure," Duckheimer scoffed as he squeezed into the passenger side. "Let's go already, Dondi. This day is officially getting on my nerves."

"On *your* nerves? Try riding in the back seat," Victoria said, letting out a disgusted chortle.

As she walked back up her new path, Eliza smiled. "Gee, Officer Krupke," was blaring.

"Psychologically disturbed, indeed," Eliza mused, greeting the inspector with wink and a nod.

She couldn't wait to mull over everything with Dr. Sylvan on Thursday.

Chapter 15

"Handcuffed in the backseat," Lois Danziger said, victoriously waving a pickle wedge she'd pinched off Poppy Sumner's plate at the counter of Soup Opera.

"Suddenly she's a pickle fan." Poppy laughed.

"You want to hear the details or not?"

"Please."

"I was there. I saw them haul her into the police station. Less than an hour ago."

"So it *was* Victoria Salinger," Poppy said, nervously shifting in her oversized red stool. She protectively slipped her left hand around her plate, shielding what was left of her veggie wrap and curly fries from Lois' grasp.

"Look who's waltzing in," Midge said, as Eliza swung through the melodic door. She hit Poppy's plate from the other end, scooping up a few fries and a decorative piece of parsley.

"Hey, get your own," Poppy said, slapping away Midge's hand. "I'm under siege here."

"Not you," Midge laughed. "Just your lunch." And with that she dove in and scored a few more fries and an errant slice of grilled yellow pepper. "So what's with the fancy hours?" Midge glanced at the clock. It was three fifteen when Eliza slid behind the working side of the counter for the first time Tuesday afternoon.

"My inspection. It was this morning. I told you."

"Oh, right, sorry. I forgot. Everything okay?"

"A-plus," Eliza beamed. She surveyed the nearly empty eatery. Aside from the loquacious trio, there was no one except Dee Dee sitting at the opposite end of the counter, her head buried in a Quimby College catalog.

"Well, you missed the excitement."

"What happened?" Eliza's eyes widened. She figured it would be a slow day. "Everything under control, Dee Dee?" she called down to her assistant.

"It was until she came in." Dee Dee shook her head––her spiky hair intact—in the direction of her mother.

"Oh, what's the drama today?" Eliza now more relaxed, grabbed a Diet Pepsi bottle from the cooler and twisted off the cap.

"Lois solved another case," Midge laughed.

"Really? Do tell."

"I didn't say I solved anything," Lois protested. "I just saw them haul the suspect in that's all."

"Suspect? Who?"

"Victoria Salinger," Midge said with a shrug. "Looks like his ex did in Hackett after all."

"I told Alex. I told Tom," Poppy said, a wistful smile crossing her face. "Statistics usually bear true."

"What were you doing at the police station anyway, Lois? Picked up for soliciting again?"

"Hilarious, Midge. Really, don't quit your day job. I was having the new waitress, Risa, fingerprinted." Ever since a murder had threatened the Goodship Inn's business and reputation last fall, Lois had been making new hires undergo stricter criminal background checks.

"Oh, right. I forgot you were running the CIA over there."

"Well, not that I want to burst anybody's bubble, but I don't think they exactly arrested Victoria. Not for murder anyway." Eliza said.

"I was there. I told you," Lois said, clucking her tongue like an annoying game show buzzer.

"I think they just brought her in for questioning," Eliza said, watching little excited bubbles waft from her soda bottle and into the stagnant barely air-conditioned air. "She was taking some stuff from Hackett's house. And they wanted to search 'her purse and person.'" Eliza smiled as she parroted Duckheimer's ominous description of Victoria's immediate fate.

"How do you know this?" Poppy asked.

"I was there. I'm moving in across the street."

"Foiled again, Lois," Midge said.

Lois, a deflated expression on her sallow, bird-like face spun around in her fuchsia gladiator sandals and stomped toward the door. "I saw what I saw." She huffed out.

"Later, Mom," Dee Dee laughed. "Much later."

"Still, they strip-searched her," Poppy said. "That has to mean something."

"I think it just means they wanted to find out what she swiped from the house," Eliza offered with a shrug.

"Anyway, why should you care if his ex-wife did it?" Midge asked.

"I don't care who did it. As long as they catch him... or *her.*" Poppy slid off her stool. "I don't care what anyone thinks of him either. He wasn't at all the way people thought. If you don't believe me, go ask Declan Rinaldi." And with that, Poppy, too, made a dramatic exit.

"I keep telling you, you'd cut down on the melodrama if you changed the name to Ye Olde Sandwich Shoppe." Midge shook her head and chuckled. She quickly grabbed a few more fries before Eliza cleared Poppy's plate, under which Midge's frazzled sister-in-law had, once again, stowed a crisp twenty dollar bill.

"Did she just say something about checking with Declan?"

"Yeah. What do you make of it?"

"Dunno. But Declan didn't seem like a big Hackett fan when I bumped into both of them at the Briar Ridge open house last month." It had only been a few weeks ago; *God how things can change,* Eliza thought, shaking off the guilt that accompanied her ebullient moving mood. "It's weird, though, I remember telling him about Hackett the day after his murder and Declan looked stricken."

"That's odd."

"Well, he said he'd seen him the night before."

"Really?"

"Yeah. He said he stopped by the station to give him a promo for the mystery movie series."

"He was at the station that night?" Midge's eyes widened to coffee-colored saucers.

"That's what he said. So I guess he was one of the last people to see him alive."

"I wonder if that's who Ethan was talking about."

"Who? What? You're holding out on me?"

"Doesn't feel so good when the shoe is on the other foot, huh?"

"Since when do I hold out on you?"

"I don't know. But I'm sure you and the Chief have a few secrets."

"He's the one with all the secrets. At least where the case is concerned."

"Very mysterious, my friend. Very mysterious indeed."

"Never mind. You're not getting off that easy. What was Ethan talking about?"

"Oh, that." Midge smiled one of those cat-that-swallowed-the-canary looks that rarely crossed her face when the two amateur sleuths were in the midst of an investigation. "I'm not sure, but Ethan told Tom and Duckheimer that some guy was having a pretty animated conversation with Hackett during the last news break of his show."

"So you think that guy was Declan?"

"Could be."

"But wouldn't Ethan recognize Declan?"

"Probably, but he said it happened so fast. He heard them arguing from the bathroom. By the time he was back at the control board, the guy was gone and Hackett was back behind the mic."

"What was the fight about?"

"I don't think he could make it out. Just heard the words 'pathetic liar.'"

"I wonder what Declan would be calling him on? Something on his show? Or maybe the way Hackett treated Ashley?

"Declan has a connection to Ashley?"

"Not that I know of, but he glared at Hackett when Ashley flirted with Hackett at the open house," Eliza said.

"So maybe Declan was upset when he found out Hackett was leading her on."

"If he was."

"Well, it's something to look into, anyway."

"Yes it is," Eliza said, biting her lip, chapped from the summer heat.

A few minutes later, Lois returned.

"Bad penny, incoming," Midge whispered with a smirk.

"Hi, Lois. Forget something?" Eliza asked, wiping down the counter.

"Yes. I forgot to mention: I also saw your brother-in-law at the station."

"Jonas?"

"Was he in imaginary handcuffs, too?" Midge asked.

"No. But it's only a matter of time," Lois snickered. "Detective Duckheimer was pretty angry. He told him he better start cooperating for real. Or there'd be 'hell to pay.'"

"Hell to pay, huh?" Midge rolled her eyes. "Sounds very dramatic. Like something out of an old Edward G. Robinson movie on TCM in the middle of the night."

"What do you want from me?" Lois asked. "I'm just quoting the man. Those were his exact words."

Chapter 16

"Sources tell the Vine, the elusive 'B' is the king—or queen—of The Quiet. Just who is this person? And is The Quiet a harmless group or dangerous cult? Tell us what you know. Keep the vine buzzing."

Eliza stared at the latest Grapevine item while WSHP's early evening show wafted through the study. "Oh, baby, look at that 'Devil in the Blue Dress' Mitch Ryder and the Dee-troit Wheels on WSHP. Speaking of Devils and villains and things that go bump in the night, don't forget to check out The Clues in the Night Film Festival at the Arts Center tomorrow night. Join the fun as they close up the whole shebang with the Agatha Christie classic, *Murder at the Gallop*."

"Declan!" Eliza said aloud, fumbling for the radio's volume button as a commercial for Goodship Honda's Labor Day Sales Spectacular boomed through the speakers. Eliza wondered what Poppy had meant earlier at Soup Opera when she indignantly defended Hackett's honor, saying, "If you don't believe me, go ask Declan Rinaldi."

"Let's throw another lid on our evening ride. Johnny B. Goode hoping you'll do the same. Stay tuned for locally rolled oldies all day, and all through the night." That sign-off was a bit of a stretch as the last local DJ of the day punched up the Kinks' classic. After the ten o'clock news, the station's oldies would be captured through a satellite dish courtesy of a network in Denver.

Hard to believe it was that late in the evening as it was still a stifling 83 degrees. And as one who hated the artificial cool of air-conditioning, Eliza rarely kept the Gordon Family Museum's mammoth system going full blast Yet, she felt a chill—one of those graveyard chills—running up her spine. Was Declan the guy who got into that "very animated" discussion with Hackett the night of the murder?

Eliza rummaged through a stack of clutter—brochures, papers, catalogs—scattered about the large mahogany desk. "Sorry, honey," she whispered with a wry laugh, knowing Eddie, a persnickety neat-freak would have abhorred the current sloppy state of affairs. Eliza would be tossing almost everything before the move next week. She'd probably take very little with her except a few books—some of Eddie's inexpensive but sentimental favorites, mostly mysteries and bios of people who died young, and the CDs they had amassed together. Most of the books were classics, some first editions, handed down from one generation of Gordons to the next. For now, they'd stay in the regal study. *It would be up to Jonas,* she thought, thinking, hoping her brother-in-law might decide to stay on, after his mysterious mission was completed.

Under a *Time* from February and the L.L. Bean Christmas Catalog, Eliza finally found the flyer for the "Clues in the Night" Summer Film Festival. Tomorrow would be the final night of the series. She and Tom had talked about going to all of them, but never went to a single showing. So much had happened in the last few weeks. The summer was nearly over, but that cloud of dread still hovered over Goodship. And it would likely remain until the Hackett murder was solved.

Feeling a sense of urgency, Eliza grabbed the phone, and with all the awkward anticipation of a teenager dialed Tom's number.

"Wanna catch a movie tomorrow night, Chief?" Eliza blurted with nervous ebullience.

"Tomorrow?" Eliza detected ambivalence and distance in that one word. "What's tomorrow?"

"Wednesday."

"Aren't you expecting a moving van?"

"That's next week."

"Oh… right." Maybe she was imagining it, but Eliza thought she heard disappointment in Tom's voice.

"It's the last night of the film series. It's no big deal. Just thought it would be fun. We don't have to go."

"Yeah, okay," Tom brightened. "We were planning to go all summer, weren't we?"

"We were indeed."

"So it's a date."

"Great. Goodnight, Tom. Get some rest."

"You, too," Tom paused. "Lovely lady."

That was that. Neither Tom nor Eliza uttered the "L" word even though they had shared a few intimate nights and clearly felt deep emotions. Eliza wondered if they could ever transcend the awkwardness. Would she always feel guilty for loving—yes she was starting to use that word to herself—her late husband's best friend? Would Tom always wince over his loyalty to Eddie?

"Time," Eliza said aloud, clutching the sleeves of Eddie's moss green cashmere sweater she had always kept draped over his high-back burgundy leather chair. "It allows us the opportunity to heal, to move on," she whispered the exact words Dr. Sylvan had soothingly uttered so many times. "Let it do its job. Work with it."

***

"Looks like it's coming to a head. Probably this weekend." Eliza's mission to secure late night snacks found Jonas talking to a girl in the kitchen.

"Do you think anyone will get hurt?" The girl, who Eliza thought looked familiar, was gnawing at her thumb.

"No, of course not. Don't worry." Jonas tapped the girl on her shoulder. "Don't flake out on me. Not now. It's almost..." The two turned around as they finally noticed Eliza heading toward the ridiculously oversized Sub Zero.

"Hi, roomie." Jonas flashed the irresistibly crooked Gordon grin.

"Hi," Eliza said, grabbing a small bottle of Poland Spring mandarin orange flavored seltzer. She recognized the girl as the plump kid who'd floated through Soup Opera, singing Jonas' praises. That was two weeks ago. *Just days before Hackett's demise.*

"Oh, hi," the girl said, turning around, meeting Eliza's smile with her own shy, braced grin.

"Don't mind me," Eliza said, aimlessly searching for munchies, discarding celery sticks as too healthy, the Rocky Road ice cream as too indulgent, the cold pizza as too desperate.

"Oh, that's okay," the girl said, a hint of nervous teenage giggle clipping her voice. "It's your house... uh...I was pretty much done, anyway." She nervously tugged at her green and white seersucker blouse that was at least two sizes too big. Eliza realized she was a cute girl and probably not nearly as heavy as her clothes made her seem.

"Don't rush on my account," Eliza smiled, settling on a container of lemon yogurt.

"Keep your ears open," Jonas said as he and the girl inched toward the door. Eliza waved, realized that despite two days worth of stubble, Jonas managed to look dapper in his olive chinos and bright blue polo shirt. A teenage girl's fantasies didn't stand a chance.

"Call me Thursday."

The girl nodded.

"And don't tell anyone."

"I think I already did," the girl said.

"Come on, I'll walk you to your car." Eliza detected just a hint of dread in his eyes, as Jonas quickly glanced in her direction.

So many mysteries, so little time. Eliza chuckled. She slipped into the breakfast nook and started unenthusiastically in on her yogurt. On the table was Jonas' briefcase—open with a manila folder labeled ICSEA peaking out. She also spied a tattered old WSHP bumper sticker. Eliza smiled. She'd never had the heart to tell Midge that Eddie hadn't much use for the local oldies outlet. But from the look of the sticker, washed out blue and green with the old (and now new) slogan "WSHP, locally rolled oldies all day and all through the night," Eliza assumed Jonas had been holding on to this souvenir from his teenage days. In the months before Hackett's murder, the station had been sporting new stickers with the slogan: "WSHP: locally rolled oldies all day; Hackett's talk every night."

"Sorry for the intrusion," Jonas said as he whisked back into the kitchen, sliding in opposite Eliza at the nook table. "Let me get this stuff out of your way." He scrambled to shove all the papers back into the well-worn briefcase and slammed it shut and placed it on the floor with a speed that somehow reminded Eliza of a kid she'd seen on *Letterman* who demonstrated how he had claimed the fastest grocery bagger's title.

"Didn't mean to interrupt anything," Eliza said with a playful smile. "But it looked like you needed a chaperone."

"Very funny," Jonas laughed. "I'm not that sort of fellow. No matter what you've heard."

"Didn't hear a thing." Eliza placed her hands over her ears.

"Cute." Jonas smiled. "Cassie's a good kid."

"She's your groupie."

"What am I? A rock star all of a sudden? I don't have groupies."

"Oh, yeah you do."

"She's just a nice girl who came to my workshop once or twice."

"Speaking of which, I always wondered what you were teaching in those workshops.

"In a nutshell: how to become independent thinkers."

"Intriguing," Eliza nodded. "So what if I asked you to go beyond the nutshell?"

"That would get pretty complicated. Wait a few days, then I think you'll understand."

"Another one." Eliza let out a sardonic chortle. "Working with Tom?"

"Not exactly," Jonas said, biting vigorously into an overripe peach, the juice splattering across his shirt and over the nook table. "Sorry." He mopped up the mess with a handful of napkins. "Did I hit you?"

"No collateral damage," Eliza quipped, helping him soak up the mess, amazed one little peach contained enough juice to wreak so much sticky havoc.

"Interesting choice of words."

"Fits in with the general tone these days."

"I guess it does." Jonas flashed his playful smile.

"Oh, did Detective Duckheimer ever track you down? I heard he was looking for you today."

Jonas' carefree expression instantly evaporated, leaving an ashen pallor in its wake. "Think we better call it a night."

Chapter 17

"Double trouble," Dee Dee said lurching out of the Soup Opera kitchen, balancing bowls of lobster bisque and black bean.

Eliza chuckled. "Good afternoon, girls," she said as Jill Dondi and her daughter Marci barreled toward the counter, the platinum blonde and midnight black of their dueling bouffants obscuring their outrageously clad figures.

"Good? Good is a stretch, girlie," Jill said, negotiating a center stool, her over-sized "I Break For Cute Shoes" tote brushing up against Miriam Sussman.

"If you don't mind," Miriam said, waving her hand like a traffic cop. She'd been nursing the same tuna wrap and bottomless lemonade for over two hours. "Some people are eating."

"Sorry," Jill said, mouthing "Your Majesty" to Eliza.

"The usual?" Eliza asked, already doling out a cup of clam chowder. She acknowledged Jill's nod just as she poured the gigantic fountain Dr. Pepper.

"Don't mind her, she's in a mood," Marci said, commandeering the stool on the other side of Miriam.

"They're gonna try and squeeze her out," Dee Dee said at the opposite end of the counter to Andy Orenstein, the owner of Aunt Hildegarde's, the funky gift shop that fed Eliza's growing bobble head habit.

"You want a mood? I'll show you a mood, "Jill said, staring somberly into the thick pottage.

"Mom, they're not interested in your melodrama. Trust me."

"Actually, that's our specialty," Eliza laughed.

"See, "Jill said, yanking on her gravity-defying black and white zebra striped boat-necked t-shirt. "It's too hot for two sizes too small," she quipped.

"For God's sake, Jill, dress for your size and age," Miriam said. "You don't have to try to impress anyone anymore."

Marci's mouth lingered agape, Eliza's eyes rolled.

"No, she's right." Jill let out a signature chortle. "But old vanity dies hard…or something like that."

"So what's your major maladjustment today?" Miriam tapped her glass and glared in Eliza's direction. Reluctantly Eliza refilled the glass with her fourth or fifth lemonade.

"She's gotta be wearing Depends," Dee Dee mumbled as she brushed by Eliza, trailing uproarious laughter as she swung back into the kitchen.

"Oh, Marci, I'm sorry. What can I get you?" Eliza sucked in her cheeks to suppress that laugh urge from emerging.

"It's really too hot for much. Just bring me the tallest iced tea you can manage.

"The flair for the dramatic runs in the family," Eliza said, filling a large glass with iced tea.

"An untrained flair, it would seem," Miriam said.

"Natural talent usually trumps formal training," Eliza said, shooting Miriam an uncharacteristic dagger look. She turned to Jill. "So what's going on, honey?"

"I'm zeroing in on that louse behind that despicable *Grapevine.*"

"Do tell," Miriam said.

"I discovered how they got a hold of those…those indiscreet photos." Jill's voice was quavering, her eyes tearing up.

"How?" Eliza asked as she deposited Marci's mammoth iced tea on her Katherine Hepburn placemat.

"*J'accuse!*" Jill waved her well-manicured shocking pink index finger around Miriam's Brillo-gray bun and in Marci's direction.

"How many times do I have to apologize?" Marci asked. I AM SORRY, MOTHER! Okay?"

"Yeah, okay. But who puts a box filled with family photographs on a table at a yard sale?"

"For the umpteenth time, I told you I didn't know there were photos in there. I just thought it was a box of old '60's t-shirts. People love that vintage crap. And you weren't exactly squeezing yourself into a Jimi Hendrix or Timothy Leary size SMALL tee shirt again in this lifetime."

"You might want to soften the apology," Eliza said.

"So how does *that* little piece of information help you zero in on the so-called louse running *The Grapevine?*" Miriam asked.

"She figures whoever bought the box of t-shirts found the Cracker Jack prize and either sold them or just posted them on *The Grapevine,*" Marci said.

"Good luck with that," Miriam sniffed. She rummaged through her straw tote, pulled out a well-worn paperback of *Sense and Sensibility.*

Eliza perked up and waved as Tom charged in, looking dapper but distracted, seemingly glued to the listening end of a cell phone conversation.

"We should start charging by the hour," Eliza said, conspicuously running a rag around Miriam's Cary Grant placemat.

"I know but…" Tom waved, transferred the phone to his opposite hand and ear. "I'm just saying if ICSEA moves in too soon….okay, Jonas. Tonight, then."

"Hi ladies," Tom beamed the forced exuberance of a man with worries on his mind. He straddled a stool at the empty end of the counter.

"This is a surprise," Eliza said, smiling. She hadn't expected him until later. And even though she knew something not so great was up, her romantic reflexes were attuned only to the bright side.

"What's the surprise?" Miriam said, glancing up from her paperback. "The man eats here every day."

"Not exactly," Eliza said, clenching her jaw. "But almost." Her affection for Tom, her spirits lifted at the very sight of him, temporarily curtailed her growing disdain for the retired librarian.

"Hit me with the chowda," Tom said in a jubilant mock Mainer accent.

"Are you really in a good mood, Chief, or is that a jovial disguise I detect?" Eliza placed a bowl of the clam pottage on his Bette Davis placemat.

"Well…" Tom's tone changed, his voice trailing into reality.

"Don't tell me," Eliza grimaced. "Tonight's a no-go."

"Sorry." Tom shook his head, looked up with that adorable boyish pout that belied his position and surely endeared the Police Chief to women of all ages and criminal culpabilities.

"I'm assuming Detective Duckheimer has something to do with this change of plans," Eliza said, though she was now certain Jonas somehow also figured into the mix.

"It won't be much longer," Tom said. "I can almost guarantee that."

"In that case, I'll try to contain my jealousy."

"Jealousy, when exercised at the right time and in the right proportion, can be a very useful barometer in relationships," Miriam offered with an authority that fetched nary a head turn.

"Who the hell asked you?" Jill said with such a sting it actually seemed to knock her off her stool. And caused an eruption laughter among what was left of the lingering late lunch crowd.

"If I waited for people to ask, no one would benefit from my wisdom," Miriam said, undeterred by the overt ridicule.

"I'm sorry, really," Tom said, staring into Eliza's liquid green eyes. "But it won't be much longer." He thought about leaping over the counter to pull Eliza into a ravenous embrace. But, as he surveyed the crowd, he realized even an afternoon kiss would be too scandalous, and instead opted for the subdued passion of an air kiss and a wink.

"Message received." Eliza laughed, blew a kiss back in Tom's direction. She found Tom's modesty amusing, albeit a little frustrating. "I'll survive. Maybe I'll entice a tall, dark stranger."

"Midge isn't so tall. And she's hardly a stranger."

"Awfully sure of yourself, aren't you, Chief?"

"No ma'am. I take nothing for granted."

Midge trampled in, her auburn hair tasseled about in a wayward charm that few women could pull off with such sporty confidence. It also signaled another humid breeze was blowing through town.

"Perfect timing." Tom nodded gleefully in Midge's direction.

"Show's over?" Eliza glanced at the lopsided clock, shocked to find the small hand had already hit the two the big one was just crawling past the ten.

"Couldn't wait to high tail it over. Practically tripped over the post of 'Who'll Stop the Rain?'" Midge laughed. "Had a hankering for your clam chowder like you wouldn't believe. Ninety degrees in the shade, and I just have to have a steaming cup."

"Music to my ears." Eliza swung into the kitchen. "Anymore chowder, Dee Dee?" she called.

"Don't tell me you're out," Midge said, biting her lip. "Not after fantasizing all day."

"Okay, I'll leave you to it, then," Tom said, waving as he headed toward the door.

"Get while the getting is good," Eliza laughed as she swung back. "You're in luck." She placed a steaming bowl of the clam chowder in front of Midge.

"I'll call you, "Tom shouted as he hit the melodic door.

Eliza wiped the counter haphazardly as she stared out the window.

"Trouble in Paradise?"

"That depends," Eliza said shaking off her perplexing reverie.

"On what?"

She waved a bottle of Diet Pepsi which Midge happily snagged.

"Busy tonight?" Eliza asked.

"It depends."

"On what?"

"What you have in mind?"

"Want to see a movie?"

"Sure. What's playing."

"Murder."

Midge spooned a delectable mouthful of the luscious chowder. "Absolutely delicious!"

Chapter 18

"They don't make 'em like that anymore," Midge said, slapping Eliza's knee. "Thank God!"

"Come on, you loved it," Eliza said. "Admit it." The two chuckled as they sprung from their cozy seats at the Goodship Playhouse. The curtain had just come down on *Murder at the Gallop*, an old Miss Marple mystery that closed out the summer mystery film series. "She was the best Marple, Margaret Rutherford. Don't you think?"

"Who am I comparing her to? Dame Edna?" Midge stretched.

"Everyone's a critic," Declan Rinaldi said, sneaking up behind them.

"Not me," Eliza said, placing a friendly peck on Declan's ruddy cheek. "I'm a sucker for the oldies."

"Hey, that's my line," Midge said, playfully alluding to her radio gig.

"Not exactly an Agatha Christie fan, Midge?" Declan asked with a whiff of incredulity.

"I wouldn't dare utter such blasphemy among the faithful," Midge said as they followed the bustling crowd through the big golden playhouse doors.

"Hey, you wanna join us for coffee? Eliza asked as they sauntered into the grand lobby. "I think we can convert her."

"Sure. Let me just square things with the projectionist." Declan ambled away with a wave.

"What are you up to?" Midge asked.

"Me? Nothing." Eliza winked. "For someone who's not a fan of murder mysteries, you're awfully suspicious."

"I'm a fan. A fan of yours. And I can tell when you're up to something."

"You want to solve *our* murder don't you?" Eliza said in hushed tones, nudging Midge just as Declan returned.

"Ready, ladies?" Declan smiled

"Always," Midge laughed. "Why don't you follow us to Sadie's."

"Where else? It's the only game in town." Declan laughed as they ambled into the parking lot. The whoosh of steamy, late summer air hit them like an uncomfortable reality check.

Midge led the way, speeding through the back roads while Eliza, thinking she should have rode with Declan, white knuckled it in the passenger seat, digging her sandaled right foot into the Volvo's maroon carpet. They were headed to Sadie's Diner; the town's only 24 hour joint which served as the default choice for snackers after 10 p.m. in Goodship.

****

"It just seemed a little too convenient the way that dead French girl didn't *look* like who she turned out to be. It's like they gave the whole thing away," Midge said, nibbling on the edge of an English muffin. "Go for the full-tilt burn next time." She scoffed, tossing the overly crisp bun on the plate.

"Easy, lady. If they start making everything to order, it could cut into my business," Eliza said.

"You've got nothing to worry about," Declan said, taking a bite from a rubbery burger. "Trust me."

"Stay open all night," Midge said. "I dare you."

"Trying to ditch me?"

"Are you kidding? I'd be in there all night. I'd be as big as a house. But between me and my husband's never-ending appetite it would be worth your while."

"So you really didn't like the movie?" Declan seemed genuinely surprised, maybe even a little hurt. Eliza couldn't decide whether she found this charming or strange. Sure he had selected the films, but so what if someone didn't care for one?

Midge shrugged, sipped her lukewarm coffee. "Even this they can't do right. Dishwater taste I can stand, but at least make it piping hot. Kills off the germs. And the taste buds."

"Midge is in a contrarian mood," Eliza said.

"Contrarian? I beg to differ." Midge let out a mock scoff laugh.

"My mother used to 'beg to differ' all the time," Eliza said. "And I'd tell her she could dispense with the begging, but if he insisted she should get down on her knees."

"Pretty sassy," Declan said.

"For twelve anyway," Eliza said, fiddling with a soggy French fry.

"So you were a smart ass?" Midge said. "Who could have guessed? Just like that pesky kid who followed Marple around in the movie."

"Maybe not *that* annoying," Eliza said.

"You really weren't crazy about it?" Declan sounded forlorn.

"It was okay. It's just…"

"She's just pre-occupied," Eliza said. "You know, with our local murder mystery."

"Oh, right." Declan sighed.

"Aren't you just dying to know what happened to Paul Hackett?" Midge perked up. "No pun intended," she added sheepishly.

"Yes. To be honest I figured if Tom and that waddling detective hadn't solved it by now, you two would have.

"Dancing as fast as we can," Midge said. "Trust us."

"Lots of twists and turns," Eliza added.

"Hackett was a tough nut to crack," Midge said, ripping open another sugar packet.

"Not if you really knew him," Declan said. "Of course he didn't let too many people in. I don't think he ever really let himself in."

"You knew him, didn't you?" Eliza asked.

Declan shrugged. "Not really."

"But you saw him that night, right?" Midge asked. "At the station. The night he was killed."

"Yeah, but just for a few minutes," Declan mumbled. "I stopped by to give him the film festival promo. It's no big secret."

"How was his mood? I mean did he seem agitated? Upset?" Midge asked.

"No. Why?" Declan slid out if his booth bench. "Look I'm not hiding anything. I told all of this to Tom and Detective what's his name."

"Duckheimer," Midge and Eliza said, eyes rolling.

"Of course you're not hiding anything," Eliza said, softly. "We're just trying to figure out if Hackett had been upset about anything."

"Or with *anyone*," Midge added.

"Couldn't tell you. I'll get this," Declan said, waving the diner check as he trudged toward the cash register.

He spun back to the booth so fast sparks were practically flying from his sneakers. "I do think he'd have been happier—for whatever time he had—if he had been honest with himself about just who he really was. For whatever that's worth."

Declan scurried to the register, paid and left without as much as a wave.

"Wow! What do you make of that?" Midge scratched her head.

"Not sure. But it seems…I mean maybe Declan was in love with Hackett." Eliza shook her head, her mind reeling back to the Briar Ridge open house. How wrong she had been crediting Declan's hostile glances at Hackett as an interest in Ashley. Now she guessed it was Hackett he'd pined for all along. "Declan's gay?"

"It's not exactly a secret." Midge laughed. "Looks like your gaydar is on the fritz, Diva!"

"Guess so." Eliza sighed. "But Hackett? He had so many women. Been married what? Two, three times?"

"Something like that. But what does that prove? Maybe he was a switch hitter." Midge took another swig of her muddy cold coffee. "Do you think Declan killed him?"

"No!" Eliza couldn't believe Declan Rinaldi was capable of murder. But then again, she guessed, anyone could give into a crime of passion given the right—or wrong—set of circumstances. "I don't know. I hope not."

"Well a lover scorned, that's one of the oldest motives."

"I doubt they were lovers," Eliza said. "I don't think it got that far."

"Unrequited love. Another oldie but goodie."

Chapter 19

"Dear God, Mom, I don't have time for this now. Just do what I told you. Trace the domain and call the Better Business Bureau." Jonas nodded and rolled his eyes as he saw Eliza float into the kitchen. "Okay. Call me back tomorrow. Get some rest. You too."

"Where angels go, trouble follows." Eliza laughed, poured a glass of grapefruit juice.

"Haley Mills. 1964?"

"I'm impressed."

"So am I. It's after midnight on a school night!" He smiled, tilted his head in the direction of the wall clock reading 12:22. "Hope you didn't do anything I wouldn't do."

"Afraid so," Eliza said, gulping down some juice. "Doubt you'd go to an old murder mystery movie with Midge or coffee with Declan Rinaldi."

"Got me there."

"So what's going on?"

"In the middle of everything, my mother is in a panic because some geriatric on-line dating service is sending her unsolicited love notes."

"Really? I thought she had—pardon the expression—something going with her boy toy golf pro."

"Yeah, and thanks for the visual, by the way. And she finds the uninvited solicitations insulting."

"I see." Eliza smiled, realizing how fond of her mother-in-law she had grown. Not that she saw her very often, since Olivia had moved to Myrtle Beach shortly after Eliza and Eddie's wedding. But their weekly phone chats had become one of Eliza's most endearing rituals. She had certainly become much closer to Olivia than her own mother.

"So instead of just deleting them like a normal person she has to make a federal case out it."

"I heard you tell her to track the domain. How would she do that?"

"The easiest way? Do a search for the domain name. If it's unavailable, you can easily trace the person or company that secured it. Then contact that person, tell them to 'cease and desist.' And if they don't, then contact the Triple B."

"Ah." Eliza's eyes grew wide.

"What are you up to?"

"Nothing. Just curious."

"Come on, I know that look."

"You show me yours and I'll show you mine."

"As inviting as that sounds."

"I didn't mean that the way it sounded." Eliza blushed.

"Think I'll go before we both get into trouble." Jonas smiled that famous Gordon family crooked grin and then brushed a light kiss across Eliza's cheek. Eliza wondered if its lingering tingle would come up in her conversation with Dr. Sylvan tomorrow.

*****

With too many questions and emotions floating in the steamy summer air, Eliza realized it would be another sleepless night. So with WSHP's satellite oldies as her late night soundtrack, she fired up the laptop and got down to business.

But just what was she searching for? *Surely the answers to Hackett's murder had to be found beyond this box,* she thought. She clicked on her favorite de-stresser, an online dice game called Farkle and electronically gambled on her ability to connect the numbers, if not the clues.

Hitchcock brushed up against the big mahogany desk, glanced up with his eager green eyes, pleading his case. "Wanna help mommy?" Eliza said, grabbing the overstuffed lovable feline fur ball and snuggling him on her lap. "You can play along." She noticed Tallulah circling the room; like a spy, the haughty calico surveyed the action, hanging back, passing judgment with her cool green eyes and accusing hiss.

"Guess a beauty like you can afford to play hard to get," Eliza said, sighing. Tallulah had always been as aloof as Hitchcock was lovable and yet Eliza still courted the calico's favor. Isn't that often the way with people, too? Though Hackett's charms remained elusive to Eliza, she couldn't deny there were many people who'd found the brash shock jock attractive. Ashley Hoyns. Poppy Sumner. His ex-wife. Maybe even Declan Rinaldi. Eliza shook her head, realizing her gaydar had become rusty since she'd abandoned the soap scene in New York City and moved to the burbs. God, she'd been so sure Declan had shot Hackett daggers at the Briar Ridge open house earlier in the summer because he had the hots for Ashley. She wondered if Hackett had returned the affection. But that was irrelevant. Midge was right: if Hackett had rebuffed Declan's advances, maybe even humiliated him in his cruel, dismissive way that could be a motive for murder.

And Declan had the opportunity. He was, after all, at the radio station the night Hackett was murdered. Stopped by, he admitted, to give him a promo for the film festival. He said he only stayed a few minutes. But Ethan heard Hackett argue with a man, said the guy stormed out. Anyway, whoever fought with Hackett left while Ethan was still there, while Hackett was still very much alive.

Was Declan angry enough to come back and confront Hackett? Maybe they got into a more vitriolic version of the fight and in a blind rage Declan killed Hackett. Anything was possible, Eliza guessed, though she still couldn't picture Declan as a murderer. And even if he was capable of murder, could he have committed this particular murder? Declan was a pretty slight guy in his late fifties. Eliza doubted he had the upper body strength to strangle someone, especially a strong man like Hackett who clearly fought back. But with adrenaline pulsating through their veins people could often perform extraordinary acts. Eliza remembered reading about a young mother who managed to lift a minivan to rescue her baby.

So? All that did was put Jill and Poppy and Ashley Hoyns and Hackett's ex-wife Victoria Salinger back on the suspect list.

"Back where I started," Eliza grumbled as with a risky roll of the Farkle dice she gambled away her 2500 point bounty.

"Epic Fail!" the ominous computerized voice admonished.

"Another county heard from," she laughed. "Heard it Through the Grapevine," the Marvin Gaye version, came on the radio.

So maybe she couldn't quite solve the Hackett case, not tonight anyway. But there was something she could do. With the information Jonas had supplied about tracing Internet domains, Eliza was determined to discover, before night's end, exactly who was behind that pesky *Goodship Grapevine.*

Chapter 20

"Talk about the cat who swallowed the canary," Tom said as he spied Eliza's satisfied grin "Guess I missed one hell of a night."

"You missed something, alright," Eliza said, leaning over the Soup Opera counter on Thursday afternoon. She stretched her long slim body to give the modest police chief more than a little peck on his chiseled cheek.

"Oh, for heaven's sake, get a room," Miriam Sussman sniped as she lifted her head from a first edition Emily Post etiquette book. She nibbled around the edges of her turkey wrap, circling the sandwich with all the discipline of a stranded camper determined to make a meager meal last for days.

"Speaking of which, I'm going to start charging by the hour." Eliza sighed, noting Miriam's current two hour tenure. Still, she berated herself for lacking the willpower to suppress her growing disdain for the nasty crank.

Midge dashed through the door, followed by Jill Dondi, who nearly tripped over her own formidable neon pink gladiator sandals.

"Did I miss anything?" Midge was breathless as she commandeered a center stool.

"Not to worry, "Eliza said. "The show has yet to begin. Let me take orders first."

"Hit me with the usual, girlie," Jill said as she sat next to Midge.

"The usual and then some," Eliza said, breaking into a whistle.

"What high octane broom did you fly in on?" Michelle Dexter said, nudging Midge and glancing at the little crooked clock which loomed precariously over the Marx Brother's poster. It was barely 2:15. "What'd you do? Put on 'Stairway to Heaven'?"

"Ah, tricks of the trade," Midge laughed. Of course, all she did was get Fast Eddie James the afternoon jock to come in a few minutes early. Partial ownership had its perks, she chuckled to herself as she zoomed over, flooring the Volvo with her usual speed. Eliza had called her earlier, promised a local fireworks display. At first she was miffed that Eliza wouldn't confide what was what on the phone, but later Midge found the mystery enticing. It gave her something to look forward to. Not that there was exactly a dearth of excitement in Goodship this summer.

"Tough crowd this afternoon," Tom said, still standing, bobbing gently in his police shoes.

"What? Are you new here?" Midge laughed as Lois Danziger pushed by, handing Midge a crinkled, bright yellow flyer as she made a beeline for an end stool. "It's like this every day."

"Oh, great," Dee Dee sighed, coming out of the kitchen, balancing bowls of black bean and cream of mushroom, as she eyed her mother.

"What's this?" Midge called over to Lois as she waved the flyer.

"Don't ask me. Those pesky things are all over town. And I nearly tripped and broke my neck on this one," Lois said, pulling on Dee Dee's arm as Eliza's young assistant tried to slip back into the kitchen. "Not so fast. I'd like a bowl of vegetable soup…if it's not too much trouble."

"I'll see what I can do," Dee Dee sighed and swung through the kitchen door.

"What's it say?" Eliza asked.

Midge read from the crumpled flyer, "Be the Voice. Be Silent now. Heed the 'B.' Listen to The Quiet."

"Another one?! You know, I almost forgot about them."

"Yep. Too bad they're not still making episodes of *Unsolved Mysteries*," Midge said, looking at Tom. "They could film a slew of 'em right here in Goodship."

"It may be ninety degrees out there," Tom said, his thumb cocked toward the window, "but in here it's getting awful cold all of a sudden."

"And the real fun has yet to begin," Eliza said.

"Doesn't look like there's any fun to be had," Miriam sniffed.

"Looks can be deceiving," Midge said.

"Among other things." Eliza doled out Jill's clam chowder.

Dee Dee popped out of the kitchen, this time with a chicken wrap for Declan Rinaldi.

"Hey, Dee Dee, did you see who put up this flyer?" Eliza asked, fondling the bright crumpled paper.

"Are you kidding?" Dee Dee barely glanced over at the flyer. "Do you know how many people traipse through here every day?"

"From your mouth to God's ears," Eliza laughed, glancing up at the ceiling.

"If they didn't, you'd be out of a job," Lois said. "And there's no room at the Inn for someone who can't even bring her own mother a bowl of vegetable soup."

"Hardee Har, old woman," Dee Dee scoffed. "Still processing your order."

"This is just getting good. Like '*Whatever Happened to Baby Jane*,'" Jill said.

"Except Jane and Blanche were sisters, not mother and daughter," Midge said. "Anyway, this isn't exactly the soap opera we paid for. What gives?"

"You didn't pay for any show," Eliza said. "Or any lunch for that matter."

"Oh, for God's sake, hit me with the soup of the day," Midge laughed. "As long as it's not the gazpacho."

"Never again!" Eliza shook her head, remembering the early summer soup of the day clunker as she doled out a bowl of clam chowder.

"Come on, what are you *not* telling us?" Tom asked. Eliza detected growing concern in Tom's usually assured, calming voice.

"Stick with me, Chief. I'll show you how it's done."

"Please, show us already," Midge said, stuffing a handful of oyster crackers into her mouth.

"I'm intrigued," Tom said, finally straddling a stool near Lois. "And just a little afraid, too."

"As you should be."

"So what's the story, girlie?" Jill asked, readjusting the sleeves on her crisp, oddly pointy pink blouse. With all systems go, she dove into her daily potage. "Delish."

"Okay, you got your audience—even if I am still waiting for one lousy cup of vegetable soup—get started already," Lois chirped.

"Well, I hope it won't be lousy," Eliza said. "Dee Dee can you bring your mom some veggie soup? Stat! Please."

"Orders are filled as we get them," Dee Dee said from the kitchen, clearly loitering to annoy her mom and maybe flirt with Sam who was working pots of navy bean and lobster bisque.

"Let's just say I had a most intriguing evening last night." Eliza glanced at Midge and Declan who was sitting at the opposite end of the counter mostly staring into a bottomless bowl of the bisque.

"Really?" Midge's eyebrows elevated in disbelief. "With all due respect to Margaret Rutherford and my companions at Sadie's, you can't be serious. I was there, and the word *intriguing* doesn't instantly come to mind."

"Ah, I guess it's all in the way you look at it," Eliza said. "Besides who says the evening ended with a kiss under the porch light?"

"I should hope not," a flushed Tom said as he cleared his throat.

"Figure of speech, Chief," Eliza said, quickly dismissing the fleeting flashback of Jonas' light, lingering kiss on her tender cheek. But she was pretty sure it would come up later in her session with Dr. Sylvan.

"Get on with it," Miriam said. "You obviously have something to announce. So announce it, for goodness sake. This opening act is not nearly as entertaining as you seem to assume."

"Oh, for God's sake," Poppy blurted from a back booth. Eliza hadn't even noticed Midge's sister-in-law sitting there incognito, her shiny bottle blonde hair tucked under a WSHP baseball cap, her tall, thin body coiled into a ball, eyes fixated on a copy of *Rolling Stone* and a barely touched eggplant Panini. "Were you born a buzz kill or did you acquire that very ingratiating skill over your long, bitter century on this earth?" Poppy pulled herself out of the booth and sauntered toward the counter.

"Excuse me!" Miriam said.

"Not so sure that's possible," Poppy said.

"I'll second that emotion," Lois said. "Might as well make myself useful while I wait for one little cup of soup."

"Coming, mother," Dee Dee shouted from the kitchen.

"This is too delicious, girlie," Jill said. "Lunch and a show. I haven't had this much fun since *Guys & Dolls* at the dinner theatre."

"And no extra charge," Midge said, glaring at Eliza. "So what gives?

"Well, I had one of those nights. You know when you're too wired to sleep," Eliza said. "So I did a little exploring on the Internet." Eliza started refilling salt shakers.

"I've got goose bumps already," Midge laughed, running her left hand up and down her bare right arm. "Simply riveted."

"Keep it up and I'll call it a day. Right here and now."

"Oh, this better be good now," Midge said, foraging around Michelle's overstuffed plate and scoring a few curly fries.

"Help yourself," Michelle said, self-consciously pulling on her oversized light green smock top. "I promised myself a summer with Jenny Craig. But that was before all this business with Phil." She was referring to the vicious rumors—reported regularly and in colorful language in *The Goodship Grapevine*—that her husband, a financial advisor and former Goodship mayor, had been implicated in a Ponzi scheme.

"No offense," Dee Dee said as she finally ambled out of the kitchen and vigorously plopped a bowl of vegetable soup on Lois' Bette Davis placemat. "But could you get to the good part?"

"Watch it!" Lois barked and jumped back off her stool. "I'm glad she keeps you on. This sort of service wouldn't fly at *The* Inn!"

"So sorry, Milady," Dee Dee said with a snicker.

"Actually, the warm-up act is getting more entertaining," Midge said. "But you may as well spill it."

"Who says I have anything to spill?"

"Come on, after all this?" Even Tom was growing impatient.

"Okay," Eliza said, letting a little salt spill onto the counter as images of Hitchcock and Tallulah's nocturnal adventures passed through her mind.

"Uh, oh, girlie. Watch it. With all that salt, we're talking bad luck for days," Jill said. "Better toss some over your shoulder or someone's going home unhappy."

"Oh, for goodness sake, only the smallest minds are consumed with such superstitious gibberish," Miriam said.

"I discovered the source of something that's been vexing the whole town all summer, "Eliza said, playing it safe with a little toss of salt over her shoulder.

"Should I summon Detective Duckheimer?" Tom asked, a startled eyebrow raised.

"Nah, I doubt he'd be interested in *The Goodship Grapevine*.

Forks and spoons clanked to attention. Even Dee Dee was curious enough to lower the melodic din of the radio.

"You found that scoundrel, didn't you girlie?" Jill was beaming. "Do tell."

"How did you do it?" Miriam asked.

"It was easy, actually," Eliza said. "So easy, I'm surprised no one figured it out sooner."

"Well, to be fair, we have been a little pre-occupied," Tom said.

"Of course," Eliza said hoping to shield his ego. "But all I had to do was trace the domain name and the person it was registered to." Eliza surveyed the enthralled counter crowd, trying to size up the reaction, gauge the inevitable fall-out.

"Well who is it?" Lois asked. "I'm still weighing my legal options." She was, no doubt, still smarting over that unflattering pic of her dashing down the street draped in a Sheer Genius smock, her hair in curlers as she ran to feed the parking meter.

"Forget it, Lois. No one *needs* to know that sleazebag's name more than me!" Jill said, fury over those naked Woodstock photos still booming through her contained contralto.

"Well, I can't be sure, of course, who did what," Eliza was hedging her bets as a sudden and misplaced wave of sympathy for the likely culprit washed over her. "But I can tell you the *Goodship Grapevine* domain is registered to M. Sussman Communications."

"What?" Jill's nostrils flared.

"Oh, this is beyond the pale." Lois shrieked.

"Not really surprising," Poppy said with a knowing nod. "To find that witch behind such a hateful site"

"You old…" Lois looked at Miriam's stool, only to find it abandoned.

Midge and Tom were rendered speechless. Dee Dee and Declan, dumbfounded, couldn't quite contain brief bursts of nervous laughter.

"*J'accuse!*" Jill blurted, sliding off her stool and lunging toward the door, where Miriam, clad in a dingy dark purple pants suit, looked small and shrunken like a discarded prune.

"All that hateful drivel about Phil," Michelle said. "What you put that poor man through. I thought he'd have a heart attack."

"My grandson, Mark," Miriam said, shielding her creased face with her straw tote bag. "I have nothing to do with it. It keeps him off the street and away from sex, drugs and rock 'n' roll. And we never posted anything that wasn't the absolute truth." She scurried out the door so fast, as she made her exit the chimes almost rang out like a helium induced cartoon character.

"Miriam Sussman and Perez Hilton," Midge said. "Who'd have thunk it?"

"Well, you've been busy," Tom said, with either pride or envy. The fact that she couldn't tell the difference was something she might want to address with Dr. Sylvan, too, Eliza thought. "Anything else you want to reveal?"

"Not yet," Eliza said, knowing full well she was no closer to solving Hackett's murder. Not that it was her job. Still, she wanted the case solved so things could get back to normal. For now, Eliza was allowing herself a moment to simply revel in this one, small victory. The fact that Miriam—or her grandson—was behind that God-awful cyber rag site made the discovery that much sweeter.

"Well, I best be getting back to work," Tom said, inching toward the door.

"I'll say," Lois said.

"Arrest that miserable Miriam," Jill said.

"Can't wait to see her in handcuffs," Poppy said. "Right there on the front page of *The Grapevine.* Such beautiful irony!"

"She should rot," Michelle said.

"Sorry, ladies," Tom said. "But I can't oblige."

"But she's a menace," Lois said.

"That may well be," Tom said, reclaiming his calm, reassuring tone. "But not according to the law. She didn't break any laws."

"So what are you saying? We have to mete out old-fashioned street justice?" Jill loomed, teetering on her gladiator sandals.

"Don't talk like that. Or you'll be the one behind bars," Tom warned with a wave of his finger.

"You looking at me, copper?" Jill said pointing her well-manicured fuchsia fingernail at Tom's chest.

"Is that your Robert DeNiro or James Cagney?" Midge laughed.

"It's my 'I didn't break any law' voice." Jill was indignant

"See to it that it stays that way," Tom said. "I don't want to have to shop around for a new place to buy my pickles and cheese."

"Don't worry," Poppy said, the first smile crossing her somber face in days. "You can always sue the wretch."

"I can't advise you on that," Tom said, winking at Eliza. "You, I'll talk to later." He waved.

"Yes, I suppose you will," Eliza said. *But not before I talk about you to Dr. Sylvan*, she thought.

Chapter 21

Still reeling from her big *Grapevine* reveal, Eliza sat in Dr. Sylvan's waiting room. She found the atmosphere, surrounded by mauve walls and punctuated by the gray and light pink accents of her couch and cushions, soothing. Much warmer than that borrowed office Dr. Sylvan used earlier in the summer.

Eliza thumbed through on old *New Yorker,* just to keep her hands busy. She could barely concentrate on the cartoons as all she had to discuss raced through her mind. The incident with Miriam and the local lynch mob was so fresh, so unnerving, she knew it would take up a large chunk of the session. *Serves me right*, Eliza thought, pangs of guilt gnawing at her. She didn't like Miriam, and that was obviously why she publicly outed her involvement in the town gossip site. But after seeing the reaction play out, Eliza actually felt sorry for the shrunken crone.

Eliza let out a laugh as she spied a cartoon featuring a guy on a shrink's couch with a caption: *"If only you told me I wasn't a people person years ago, I could have saved all this money and could actually enjoy hating people."*

She wasn't sure why she was laughing. It wasn't particularly funny. But it said something about this therapy business. Not to mention what actually makes people happy. She'd want to bring up those new suspicions swirling around Declan and the whole Hackett murder, though she knew Dr. Sylvan would rather not hear it. If it wasn't directly about her life, Dr.

Sylvan thought Eliza was wasting her time, using superfluous events as a way to avoid her own life decisions. Maybe so. But the murder hovered over not only Goodship, but her stalled relationship with Tom. And besides, it was intriguing. There was no getting around it, Eliza, much to Tom's chagrin, enjoyed sleuthing. And there was Jonas' kiss. Eliza had tried to swat it away, but it lingered, looming like a harbinger of something—*what?*—to come.

The waiting room door opened and Eliza was startled by an odd nasal voice singing, "There's a Kind of Hush All Over the World."

Eliza looked up to discover Carl, that strange young man from the nature center, the same odd guy who blared the "Sounds of Silence" at the edge of her gate, dropping one of those weird 'Be Quiet,' flyers.

"Oh, sorry," Carl said, something akin to a reddish tint blotching his strikingly pale face. "Didn't know anyone was in here."

"No problem. Hi," Eliza said, smiling, wondering if he recognized her.

He just offered a wan smile and sat in a chair across the room, crossing and re-crossing his long, thin legs.

Speaking of mysteries, that new Quiet flyer stirred interest in that little diversion. Eliza couldn't figure out why, but she suddenly had a nagging feeling The Quiet business and the Hackett murder may be connected. *But how?*

Dr. Sylvan popped out of her office. She looked especially buoyant, wearing a bright orange and pink batik blouse, a color scheme that was more vibrant than the therapist's usual muted palette and one that brought out the luminosity of her bright blue eyes and shiny silver pixie hair.

"Come in, Eliza," Dr. Sylvan said, ushering her into the office. "I'll be right with you."

Eliza plopped into her usual perch on the comfy oversized gray chair. Dr. Sylvan returned to the waiting room. Presumably to deal with Carl, who Eliza assumed was another patient, probably with a scheduling conflict or maybe a crisis. She hoped she wouldn't be the one who'd have to reschedule. Not that what she had to discuss could in any way be construed as a crisis, but she was anxious. About so many things.

She heard snatches of the muffled waiting room conversation, but couldn't make out much, only phrases: "highly inappropriate" and "not the time for this" and "dangerous mistake," coming from Dr. Sylvan's voice, tinged now with an uncharacteristic ire. That last one piqued Eliza's interest. What dangerous mistake was this strange young man about to make? Or did he make it already?

Eliza pushed herself up in the comfortable chair, aligning her spine in a posture of punctuality and prudence. Not that she was ever summoned to the principal's office; as a child actor she had been schooled mostly on the set, but imagined the sensation she was experiencing came close to such trepidation. For some reason, she thought she better get her story straight.

****

"Well, surely you expected that reaction," Dr. Sylvan said, a slight note of admonishment in her voice.

"I'm not sure what I expected."

"Really? You knew these women were upset about things *The Grapevine* had been running all summer. And you said none of them were particularly fond of Miriam Sussman."

"Yeah, well, that's true." Eliza bit her lip like a nervous little kid.

"So you assembled them there."

"I wouldn't go that far. I wouldn't say I assembled anyone."

"Summoned? Is that a better word?"

"Not really. The only one I came close to *summoning* was Midge. I did call her and told her I had something to announce."

"But you knew the others would be there, right? They were part of your usual audience."

"I guess. I mean they are usually at Soup Opera about that time. Well, Jill and Lois anyway."

"Fine. So—semantics aside—you were pretty confident you'd have your desired audience for the shocking announcement. Fair to say?"

"Fair to say," Eliza conceded, staring at her beige Nubuck sandals, noticing, for the first time, how badly scuffed her right heel looked, wondering just how long she'd been schlepping around like that.

"So is it also fair to say that you were hoping to elicit—shall we say—a *dramatic* reaction?"

"I don't know," Eliza said, that guilty pang gnawing away at her again. "I guess I did."

"And now you feel guilty about it?"

"Maybe it's guilt or..."

"Or?"

"I don't know. Maybe I just feel a little sorry for Miriam. She looked so small, so diminished."

"Do you think she brought any of it on herself?"

"Yes, of course, but..."

"But what?"

"She looked so exposed."

"And *you* exposed her."

"Right." Eliza muttered.

"And now you feel bad about that?"

"Yeah, I guess. A little."

"Don't you think Miriam deserved to be exposed, to be held accountable for the things she posted, said, wrote whatever they call it on those blogs?"

Eliza shrugged. She looked at Dr. Sylvan, sensing the therapist's growing impatience with the subject. "Yes, but maybe not that way."

"What would have been a better way?"

"I don't know," Eliza said. "If I thought of it, I probably would have done it that way." She threw up her hands.

"Well, it's done."

"Right. But that doesn't mean I have to enjoy it so much."

"It doesn't sound like you enjoyed it at all."

"Oh, but I did."

"It would seem the fun was short lived."

"Yeah."

"So what have you learned from this? Anything?"

"I'm not sure. I guess that there are two sides to everything. And at least two ways to feel about most things too." Eliza wondered if her answer sounded as tentative, as childish as she felt.

"Can you accept that and let Miriam deal with her own well-earned consequences and move on?" Eliza thought she heard that tinge of ire again.

"I guess I'll have to."

"Fine. Then let's move on, with what time we have left, to something more relevant to *your* life."

Eliza wasn't really ready to let go of *The Grapevine* guilt, but Dr. Sylvan had a way of steering the session, moving things along in a way that she assumed was therapeutically motivated. Or was it merely a way for Dr. Sylvan to negotiate her own threshold for boredom? She had seemed, to Eliza, increasingly distracted, even disinterested in the last few weeks of the summer.

"Why is this not important? It just happened today, and it's weighing on my mind."

"I know it is," Dr. Sylvan's warm voice was now coated with its sagacious signature. "But we've exhausted it. It's time to put it away, if just for today. Let it settle in and next time we'll see just how important it remains. Sound reasonable?"

"Yes, I guess so," Eliza reluctantly agreed. "So what do you want to me to talk about?"

Dr. Sylvan shook her head, her pixie hair swaying like a curtain in a summer breeze. "You've been coming here long enough to know that's not the way it works."

But Eliza, knowing that's precisely the way it worked, brought up Hackett's murder, watched as Dr. Sylvan quelled a grimace as it crept onto her kind face. "They don't seem any closer to nabbing the culprit. And it's almost been two months."

"So? I still don't understand why the murder of a man you barely knew—and one you admittedly didn't like—should occupy so much of your time and concern."

"Well, it is upsetting," Eliza said with a sigh. "And intriguing."

"And it's a distraction from your own life."

"Maybe, but it's not like it's completely unrelated to *my* life."

"How is it related?"

"Well, the investigation has helped stall my relationship with Tom."

"I was afraid of that."

"It's like we're stuck in a perpetual stop-and-start pattern." Eliza said. "I'm not sure we can get out of it."

"Do you want to get out of it?"

"Of course," Eliza heard the forced indignation in her own voice. "Well one way or another. It can't go on like this forever."

"Maybe you're spending too much time talking about it!" Dr. Sylvan's voice couldn't contain her growing agitation. "That's what people do: Talk, talk, talk! As if that alone could solve anything."

Eliza, at first, bristled at those words, such a bizarre admonishment from a therapist whose life's work was words and feelings and their underlying meaning. But then she saw the clarity, the wisdom, behind it. "You're probably right." Eliza laughed. "I just never thought a therapist would say it like that."

"I know. I'm sorry," Dr. Sylvan said, a wry grin on her face as she slapped herself lightly across the mouth. "I shouldn't have put it quite that way. But sometimes you can lose your patience with patients." She laughed at her own tired therapist's chestnut.

"I bet." Eliza laughed, too. It was a little unnerving, but also refreshing to see her therapist have such an unrehearsed human moment.

"Talking is therapeutic, of course. I know all too well the healing power of this process, but eventually it has to lead to action."

"Of course. That's the whole point."

"So what do you want to do about Tom?"

"I don't know. That's the problem."

"Well, what do you think it will take for you to know what action you will need to take to either move this relationship forward or let it go."

Let it go? The sound of those words made Eliza's heart sink. She certainly wasn't ready to let go of whatever she had with Tom. But was she truly ready to move forward? Eliza just shrugged.

"Well, this is where you clearly need to focus your energy."

"I guess so," Eliza said. "Oh, I almost forgot: Jonas kissed me. The other night."

Dr. Sylvan's penciled-on gray eyebrows rose to attention. "Your brother-in-law kissed you, and this is the first you're mentioning it?"

"It wasn't on the top of my mind," Eliza lied. "And it was only on the cheek. But…"

"But what?"

"The feeling it left…I can't quite shake it…the sensation lingered for days."

"So there seems to be yet a new character in the mix."

"Yes, I guess there is." Eliza was actually surprised at how blithely she agreed with that assessment.

"And despite your protestations to the contrary, you do seem to possess a flair for the dramatic," Dr. Sylvan said, an intrigued smile lighting her face. "Unfortunately your timing needs work. Our time is up. We'll have to leave it there today."

"Okay," Eliza said, gathering her bag and launching off the comfy mound of a chair. "I'll see you next week."

"Oh, did I forget to mention, I'll be away for the next few weeks? I'll be back the end of September."

"No. But I figured if you missed August, as a shrink you were out of luck." Eliza laughed.

"I'm always a step behind." Dr. Sylvan laughed, offered her long, weathered hand to Eliza.

"Well, you certainly deserve a vacation. Listening to other people's problems must take its toll."

"More than you know." Dr. Sylvan walked Eliza to the door. "But you're not off the hook, my dear. Do your homework. By the time we meet again, I'll want to hear your plans."

"I'll do my best," Eliza promised with a smile.

"That's all we can ask," Dr. Sylvan returned with her warm smile and a comforting pat on the back.

Chapter 22

"Maybe she should spend her vacation in the loony bin." Midge laughed that mischievous girl laugh that belies encroaching middle age. She swiped another handful of licorice nibs from the complimentary Soup Opera canisters.

"Stop!" Eliza put her hand up, her mock traffic cop pantomime.

"Hey, I can't help myself. They're addictive." Midge slipped one errant candy into her mouth. "You're like a dealer. Enticing us with free samples...they're still free, right?"

"For now." Eliza laughed. "Of course, help yourself. But knock off the jokes." Eliza was distracted, her eyes darting between Midge and the back booth where Tom, Detective Duckheimer and—of all people—Jonas were huddled, talking in hushed tones as they scarfed down turkey and avocado, ham and cheddar, and tuna and cranberry wraps. She suspected Jonas was in on the investigation, but she hadn't been able to nail down the how or why.

"Don't go soft on me. Please," Midge said. "There are too few people in this town with any sense of adventure."

"I'm not. But it's not right...making jokes like that. It's probably unethical even,"

"That's the other way around," Midge scoffed. "It's unethical for a therapist to talk about her patients, but I'm pretty sure they're fair game. Anyway, Sunny Sylvan has it coming."

"I wouldn't say that." Eliza shook her head, regretting mentioning Dr. Sylvan's snippy mood, her almost dismissive comments. *Should have let well enough alone*. After all, Eliza was still deciding whether to continue with her and if she did, she wouldn't want to have to justify it to Midge.

"Actually, she's helped me a lot. On more than one occasion." Eliza rubbed her neck. Craning her neck was doing a number on her. Another hazard of this sleuthing business.

"Right. But she hasn't cured you of your affliction yet."

"Which is?"

"You're distracted by shiny objects." Midge spun around her oversized stool, waving at the three men.

"Stop it!" Eliza swatted her hand at Midge. "You're incorrigible. Like an overgrown teenager"

"That's only because you keep plying me with free candy, pusher." Midge grabbed a handful of Tootsie Roll midgies out of the canister nearest her reach. "I see the boys are back in town." She laughed, singing part of the chorus of the old '70's hit.

"Think I'll go be a fly on the wall," Eliza said as she slipped around the counter and headed toward the back. "Just remember you drove me to it."

"So you're saying Monday is D-Day? That means we better move on this now," Detective Duckheimer said.

"Can I get you anything, gentlemen?" Eliza smiled brightly as she happened upon the intriguing tidbit. She quickly darted her eyes from Jonas to Tom and finally landed her gaze on Duckheimer, who was shaking ham and cheddar wrap crumbs from his bushy mustache. "Another round of sodas. Or maybe a couple of clues?"

"Ah, there's that thespian humor again, Mrs. Gordon. Really, you shouldn't waste it on me."

"No extra charge," Eliza said, gritting her teeth.

"We're fine," Tom said, a pleading look in his blue eyes.

"Actually, we need all the help we can get." Jonas smiled that alluring crooked Gordon grin.

"Come on, Gordon. We don't have time for amateur antics," Duckheimer said with his infamous scowl. "But a cup of coffee would be nice."

"Coming right up." Eliza forced a smile. "Coffees all around?" All three men nodded dismissively.

Eliza discovered a flurry of unexpected activity when she returned to the counter. A new couple, middle-aged and clad in matching pink and orange madras plaid Bermuda shorts and light green Polo shirts had snagged the table near the window. And Dandy Dave McKenna, WSHP's morning DJ, was standing next to Midge, waving a stack of bumper stickers.

"We seem to have more supply than demand," Dave joked in the same rich baritone he used on the radio.

"Those are evergreen. Let's concentrate on unloading those damn beach balls and towels," Midge instructed.

"Beach Blanket Bonanza!" Dave bellowed.

"Hey, I know someone who'd love to have one of those." Eliza snagged a bumper sticker from Dave's large hand.

"Fans? We actually have fans?" Midge chortled.

"Well, at least one, Eliza said. Then she bounced back to the detective booth with a tray of coffees.

"So, Saturday. Agreed?" Jonas said as Eliza approached the booth. "I mean we have to move. They're getting increasingly militant and dangerous."

"Okay, okay," Duckheimer said, holding up his hand as he saw Eliza.

"Thanks," Tom said with a wink. Maybe he wasn't annoyed with her, after all.

"You're very welcome, Chief."

"That'll be all, Mrs. Gordon," Duckheimer said, his piercing brown eyes shooting off dismissive rays.

"Oh, I thought you'd like this." Eliza ignored Duckheimer's dismissal as she deposited the crisp WSHP bumper sticker on Jonas' Jimmy Stewart placemat.

Jonas smiled. "Oh, wow. Cool," he said. "How'd you know I collect them?"

Eliza returned the smile. "I have my sources."

"I'll bet." Jonas smiled.

Tom shifted uncomfortably and Duckheimer shot Eliza a few more dismissive daggers. And so she decided to saunter back to the counter in search of warmer climes.

They're militant and increasingly dangerous. The words reverberated in Eliza's head. The investigative trio had to be talking about the Hackett case, right? So now there was a *"they"* in play? There was more than one culprit? And if they were *militant* and *increasingly dangerous,* she doubted the group could be comprised of any variation of the growing suspect list of Jill, Declan, Poppy, Ashley and Hackett's ex-wife. They hardly seemed conspiratorial or militant, let alone increasingly dangerous. So who were the *they* the detectives were so concerned about? Some sort of organized group—a militant, dangerous group of thugs who ran around killing obnoxious radio hosts? Clearly something was missing; and whatever that was continued to elude Eliza's grasp.

"Excuse me," the new man at the window table said, clearing his throat and rapping his knuckles on the table. "Do you offer table service or do we have to order at the counter?"

"Oh, sorry," Eliza said, shaking off her sleuth sloth, as she meandered to their table. "What can I get you?"

"Do people really order soup?" The woman asked, flashing a neon-white veneer smile.

"Well, that is our specialty," Eliza said, in no mood for friendly banter about the wretched weather.

"I assumed as much. But with the blasted heat I just wondered."

"We have a full line of sandwiches, too." Eliza grabbed a menu from the counter and handed it to the woman.

"Of course they say hot soup will cool you off in the heat," the man said. "Isn't that right? Surely you've heard that too."

"Heard it and happily spread that rumor every chance I get," Eliza said, now getting back into the small talk swing.

"Oh, that's just an old wives' tale, isn't it?" the woman said.

"All I can tell you is a lot of folks come in and eat hot soup here every day, even in the summer. Thank God."

"Well, you sold me," the man said. "Give me a bowl of the New England clam chowder."

"Make it two," the woman said. "We're practically in New England, aren't we?"

Eliza nodded. "A few miles up the road." She went into the kitchen to ladle out the chowders.

The bowls deposited, Eliza slipped back around the working side of the counter where she faced Midge's incredulous glances.

"What's with you?" Midge asked. "You seem so out of it. I mean it's not like you have to unload 50,000 beach balls this weekend."

"At least the stress hasn't infringed on your ability to exercise hyperbole," Eliza said, flinging a rag in Midge's direction.

"In times of duress, we cling to what we know."

"Wish I had a talent to cling to."

"Oh, come on. Don't go fishing today, genius, it's too darn hot."

"I'm not fishing," Eliza said, with a dismissive wave.

"Really, I'm just in a funk, I guess. Just not in the mood to make nice with late day quasi tourists, I guess."

"I hear ya," Midge said, glancing at the couple. "But they look harmless enough"

"So did Paul Hackett."

"Not really." Midge let out a deep, sardonic chortle.

"Okay, bad example," Eliza conceded.

"And more than we can say about the Three Musketeers." Midge tilted her head toward Duckheimer, Tom and Jonas as they ambled up to the register.

"All set?" Eliza asked without making eye contact with either Tom or Jonas; instead she fixed her gaze, once again, on Detective Duckheimer. Although his jovial appearance defied his grumpy, no-nonsense demeanor, something about the man amused Eliza, lightened her mood.

"Yes, Mrs. Gordon. Thanks." Detective Duckheimer locked his stern brown eyes on her quizzical green eyes, as he settled the check.

"That's gotta be a first, huh?" Jonas backslapped Duckheimer and laughed.

"I always pay my way, Mr. Gordon." Duckheimer walked to the door, a trail of crumbs and his signature rubber soled shoe quacks punctuating his exit.

"The County has a pretty generous expense voucher plan," Tom said. "Call you later," he whispered with a wink.

"Please." It was all Eliza could muster. Something was going to go down. She could feel it. She knew they were finally closing in. And now she wondered, worried if *they* were *militant* and *dangerous* enough to harm anyone else. Could they, would they harm Tom? Or Jonas?

"Snap out of it!" Midge snapped her fingers in Eliza's face.

Eliza flinched. "What? Snap out of what?"

"Your—I don't know what—semi-fugue state."

"I'm not that out of it," Eliza said, trying to focus, fixating her eyes on the new *North By Northwest* poster she'd hung on the wall across from the counter last week. "Does that look centered?"

Midge shook her head. "More centered than you."

"Okay, back to business," Eliza said as she wandered over to the middle-aged couple's table.

"Delicious," the woman chirped.

"And I think it works. I really do," the man said. "I'm starting to feel cooler already."

"I'm glad you're enjoying the chowder, but I doubt it accounts for your cooler temps. You can thank the A/C for that." Eliza pointed to the vent right above their table. "You folks new in Goodship? I don't think I've seen you around before."

"Yeah, we're from Richmond," the woman said, a sudden Southern hint coating her voice. "Zach's company transferred him to the New York office."

"Digital Business Solutions," Zach beamed.

"Don't get him started or he'll talk high tech geek all night," the woman offered with a clipped laugh that seemed to chip away at their sunny appearance.

"Let's not forget: it's that high tech geek that brought you up to New York." The man held out his hand. "Zach Royce. This is my wife Bonnie."

"I'm Eliza Gordon." Eliza shook Zach's hand, impressed by his firm confident grip.

"Pleased to meet you." Bonnie smiled, offering a flash wave.

"If Bonnie had her druthers we'd live in the City, but I figured it would be too much of a culture shock 24/7."

"And the high school has a great reputation," Bonnie said. "We have a fifteen year old son, Ollie. He'll be a sophomore."

"My daughter Hannah's going into her senior year. God help us, we have college applications to look forward to."

"It's such an exciting time."

"Oh, I'm Midge Sumner, by the way." Midge reached over and shook hands with Bonnie and then Zach. Then she deposited a pair of WSHP bumper stickers on their table.

"Thanks."

"Midge is also the local radio star," Eliza said.

"More like workhorse and co-owner," Midge demurred in a rare moment of modesty. "And Eliza is a former soap star and the usually ebullient proprietor of this cozy establishment."

"Well, imagine that," Bonnie said, another flash of those veneers Eliza figured she'd adjust to.

"You know we walked by the station that night," Zach said.

"The night of the murder," Bonnie added, whispering *murder* in such a hushed tone she was practically mouthing the dangerous word.

"We were walking Bugsby," Zach said.

"That's our little Bichon. Retired show dog. Finished third at Westminster three years ago."

"Sounds adorable." Eliza winked at Midge.

"Positively. And don't think he doesn't know it." Bonnie chuckled.

"The most spoiled member of the family," Zach said. "Except for his mommy, of course."

Bonnie smiled and punched Zach affectionately on the shoulder. *Oh, these two are too cute*, Eliza thought.

"We walked up that big hill and followed that bright light," Bonnie said.

"Bugsby was very attracted to that light," Zach added.

"My brother's obsession with security," Midge sighed. "Ironic isn't it?"

"We heard about it the next day," Zach said.

"Shocking and so sad," Bonnie said.

"But I take it he—Hamilton was it?" Zach asked

"Hackett," Midge and Eliza mumbled.

"I gather he wasn't exactly beloved around here."

"That, sir is the understatement of the decade," Midge said.

"I'm guessing you weren't terribly fond of him yourself."

"Not even a little fond," Midge said. "But he did work for our station and he used to be my brother's friend."

"I think we get the picture. Sort of a Glenn Beck loud mouth type, this fella?" Zach leaned back in his chair and closed his eyes, revealing luscious light brown lashes Eliza knew would curry envy among many women.

"If Glenn Beck had a baby with Howard Stern that would be Paul Hackett," Midge said.

"With Rush Limbaugh as the grandpa," Eliza added.

"A most disagreeable sort?" Zach said.

"Still, I'm sorry for your trouble," Bonnie said, coating her comment with a healthy slather of Southern Comfort. "But it sure is fascinating watching it from the outside looking in."

"Of course most folks in that position are content to sit silently watching from the sidelines." Zach said, he too, now punctuating his accent in Southern shades.

"Look who's talking," Bonnie said. "You're just as bad."

"I guess I am." The pair then flashed those neon veneers and let out a synchronized, measured laugh that sounded well-rehearsed.

"We're not famous for shutting our big fat mouths around here either," Midge said, nudging Eliza.

"Though there are a few people trying to change that." The Quiet and her encounters with that strange Carl guy ran through Eliza's mind. *It's all connected*, she thought. *But how?*

"Trust me, it'll never take," Midge said. "Not in this town."

"Life is for the loud and proud," Zach said, offering an odd fist bump, incongruous to his middle-aged preppie look.

"You can say that again," Midge said.

Chapter 23

Jonas, hunched over the granite island, papers splayed across the counter, eyes riveted on his work, was oblivious to Eliza's light-footed entrance.

"We've got to stop meeting like this," Eliza said as she brushed by him on her way to the fridge. She noticed a memo with ICSEA emblazoned at the top. She'd seen that word—or was it an acronym?—before.

"Oh, hi," Jonas said, startled. Eliza fetched a bottle of Diet Pepsi from the refrigerator. "Want one?"

"Yeah, okay," Jonas said, clearing his throat. "Guess I am a bit parched." He flashed that Gordon grin.

"Don't worry, in a few days you won't have to put up with my intrusions anymore." Eliza smiled as she tried to casually rub up against his paperwork.

"You have that backwards, don't you?"

"Well, I guess it's how you look at it." Eliza strained to find more clues in Jonas' mélange of top secret clutter. "Either way, we won't be having these late-night trysts."

"Go ahead: abandon me! I should be used to it by now." Jonas pouted. Eliza realized that was a cute countenance on him, too.

"I could give you the number of a good therapist."

"No, thanks. I've been down that road."

"In that case, you should be able to 'process' your feelings."

"Sounds like you've been drinking the Kool Aid."

"Nah, just sipping it."

"Be careful."

"You too."

Jonas' penetrating chocolate brown eyes registered surprise "Careful about what?"

"I don't know." Eliza shrugged. "Things that go bump in the night?"

"Especially once you leave me alone in this big old house."

"You'll get over it. You'll fill it with something...or someone...in no time."

"Don't be so sure."

"Flatterer!" Eliza laughed, playfully punched Jonas' emerald green polo clad shoulder. "How 'bout you give me a going away present."

"Name it." Jonas smiled. *Irresistible?* Eliza bit her lip.

"Tell me what you're up to?"

"That's an easy one," Jonas said, knowing his answer wouldn't put an end to Eliza's inquiry. "Just paperwork."

"Not so fast," Eliza said, leaning her back against the counter. "I mean what's *your* involvement with Tom and Duckheimer's investigation into the Hackett murder?"

"Can I plead the fifth?"

"I'd rather you didn't."

"And playing dumb is out of the question?"

"Think it's a little late for that."

Jonas gnawed on his lip, lowered his head in a ponderous gaze. "Where to begin?"

"Maybe start with Ick-Sea?" Eliza blurted, almost beaming with schoolgirl exuberance.

Jonas, his eyes widening, jumped off his perch. "You are good." He glanced at the ICSEA file amid his paper jumble.

"It's part of this, right?"

Jonas shrugged. "Yes and no."

"Come on, guy. I didn't go to dental school."

"Losing your cool, Mrs. Gordon?" Jonas laughed.

"Don't pull a Duckheimer." Eliza laughed. "Just answer my questions, Mr. Gordon."

"Talk about pulling a Duckheimer, lady."

"You said 'name it.'"

"So I did." Jonas paced around the kitchen, his bare feet gliding on the cool, marble floor. "Okay here goes: ICSEA is the International Commission on Subversive and Exploitive Activities."

"Whoa…that has, I don't know, a Joseph McCarthy ring to it."

"Not quite," Jonas said. "It's a shadow agency— mostly comprised of American, British and European agents monitoring and infiltrating dangerous groups."

"You're talking terrorist cells?"

"Sometimes." Jonas shook his head. "It depends how you define terrorism, I guess. What we primarily deal with are organizations that engage in brainwashing and dangerous group think."

"You mean cults?"

"Sometimes."

"This is a government agency?"

"It's not the FBI or CIA. But ICSEA often works in tandem with them."

"But people are free to join cults, right?"

"Of course. But when the activities of the groups, cults, whatever you call them, become criminally injurious of their members or the public at large law enforcement has to step in to avert such activities."

"That sounds like government mumbo jumbo."

"You asked."

"I did," Eliza laughed, tilted her head, seeing Jonas in a whole new light. "So you're an ICSEA agent?"

"Got me."

"So you really are an International Man of Mystery."

"Guilty, I guess." He laughed.

"How did you get into this? And why didn't you tell anyone about it?"

"As to the first part of your question: it's a long story." Jonas paused, stared pensively into the air.

Eliza, sensing a tonal shift, slipped into the dining nook. She waited, hugging the mauve back cushion, giving Jonas time to conjure past secrets, gauge their significance and decide which—if any—he might share with his sister-in-law.

"I guess it won't come as a shock to learn it started with a girl," Jonas finally said.

"Not really," Eliza said without a scintilla of sarcasm or jocularity.

"It was, I guess, about twelve years ago now, right after college. I did that aimless summer tour thing, landed in London with a few blokes. One of the guys had a sister—a beautiful girl, red-head, big personality, very sexy. And talented, too—she won a prestigious scholarship to RADA." Jonas sighed, looked wistful.

"I'm impressed," Eliza said, hoping to keep the story moving.

"We had I guess what you'd call a whirlwind romance."

"I get the picture."

"Really, I've had girlfriends before but...I mean...well, I guess I fell in love. Hard and fast." Jonas paced around, glanced out the big picture window as if he'd find some lost treasure in the summer night's sky.

"Sounds beautiful," Eliza said, regretting the words as they slipped from her lips. Obviously, it didn't end well; Jonas already looked emotionally drained.

"It was. For about three months," Jonas said, now sliding in opposite Eliza in the dining nook bench. "I decided to stay. So I played around like any trust fund trash; toyed with running an art gallery with one guy;

an indie record label with another. But it was all about Megan. Wanting her, being with her, dreaming about our future."

"You were going to marry her, weren't you?" Eliza looked into Jonas' watery chocolate brown eyes.

"Well, we were talking about marriage, babies, the whole shebang. It's hard to believe, I know, but I wanted that...with her...desperately."

"Not so hard to believe." A wistful flash of those babies she'd so yearned for with Eddie ran through Eliza's mind. "She didn't want to get married?"

"At first she did. But something happened that winter. She flubbed an audition for a new play on the West End and it just shot her confidence. She started losing out on parts in college, too. She got depressed. I mean serious 'can't get out of bed' depressed. She stopped going to her classes, she wouldn't eat, sleep. She wouldn't even let me come over. Even stopped taking my calls."

"I'm sorry. Did she get some help? Maybe see a counselor?"

"I suggested it, of course. Her roommate, her friends, they all tried. But she just shut us all out." Jonas shifted his body, looked out the window. Eliza thought he might bolt out of the nook. But he didn't.

"Then one day, maybe two or three weeks later, she called, sounded so cheerful. She did a complete 180, said everything was great. She said she had found 'The Way.'"

"The *Way?* To what?" Eliza asked, already getting the culty, brainwashed picture.

"That's what I asked." Jonas shook his head, a tentative smile crossing his face. "She went into this whole spiel, sounding cloyingly perky, almost manic, about spiritual enlightenment and healing growth. Said she found the answers when a friend—another acting student—took her to a weekend seminar and a guru named Simeon taught them to follow *The Way*."

"So she joined a cult."

"Two days." Jonas snapped his fingers. "Two days is all it took to get her swept up into that nonsense, the group think."

"Well, obviously she was at a vulnerable point in her life." Eliza shook her head, thought about touching Jonas' hand, but decided to leave him in his own space.

"Yeah." Jonas nodded. "She told me she was done with the 'confines of conventional thought and living' and was following Simeon to his cloistered community."

"Obviously you tried to talk her out of it."

"Of course. God, I loved that girl so much I would have traveled the world over just to be with her."

"She didn't want you to?"

"She wouldn't even tell me where it was. She said if I was meant to follow that same path, I'd instinctively find my way to *The Way*."

"Wow."

"Yeah. She was real far gone." Jonas looked into Eliza's green eyes, falling into them, remembering Megan, but appearing to lose some of the pain at the same time.

Eliza shook her head. "After only a couple of days. That's disturbing."

"I was so stunned. I didn't know what to do. But I knew I couldn't just let her go."

"What did you do to try to stop her?"

"I begged, pleaded. That didn't work, of course. So I tried to follow her. But *The Way* was quite cagey. They didn't exactly print up maps and brochures for tourists."

"You mean they deliberately make it hard for folks to find *The Way*. Seems like a lot of intrigue for a cult."

"You'd be surprised what these so called 'gurus' will do to 'protect' their followers from negative or toxic influences."

"And that would be family members, friends…"

"Basically anyone who didn't drink the Kool-Aid."

"Knowing you, I'm guessing that wasn't the end of it."

"Of course not. I did everything I could think of: pumped all her friends and family for clues, tracked down friends of the friend who dragged her to that meeting, eventually I hired a private detective. After a month or so he got me in touch with a guy who knew a guy who ran the British ICSEA office."

"Hmm…so you were recruited."

"Eventually. First, I was just interested in getting to Megan, knocking some sense into her, bringing her home."

"Very romantic…in a caveman sort of way."

"In a very desperate caveman sort of way," Jonas sighed. "After much cloak and dagger business, the ICSEA honcho, Gregory Chisolm—who by the way was out of central casting, looked very James Bond—and I finally found *The Way* compound in a small isolated town in Northern Wales."

"So was she there?"

"Yes and no." Jonas hung his head. "She was there but she wasn't Megan anymore. The girl I knew, the girl I was in love with had been replaced by a cheerful, vapid robot. It was like *The Invasion of the Body Snatchers*. She even changed her name. Now she was called Cloud."

"I'm so sorry."

"It was devastating."

"I'm so sorry," Eliza said again with a somber nod. "Was she happy to see you?"

"Well, yeah, in that crazy, placid sort of way. She blathered on about serenity and the authentic universal consciousness. All that group think b.s."

"Did you try to get her to leave?"

"Sort of. But there was no penetrating the 'mystic wall.' There was no point. And really no chance."

"What do you mean?"

"There were cultists roaming around, watching our every move, listening to our every word."

"So they kicked you out?"

"Not exactly." Jonas stared out the window. "She said 'I wish you the expansive love of the universe,' and gave me a peck on the cheek. Then she skipped off with another pair of brainwashed clones. That was the last time I saw her."

"I'm sorry. It must have been so painful for you."

"Yeah." Jonas nodded, grimaced.

"So that's how you got into cult busting. You were recruited by that James Bond guy?"

"Gregory," Jonas laughed. "I guess he recruited me. It was pretty informal at first. I was crushed by Megan, but it sort of jolted me into action. I couldn't just play around. I was so incensed at what these people had done to her. And Gregory convinced me there were ways to help save other vulnerable people. He taught me about tracking and infiltrating, even a bit of de-programming and re-education."

"Ah, so that explains those 'personal growth workshops.' You were recruiting kids, right? But for what?"

Jonas laughed. "Don't get ahead of yourself. See you're pretty intrigued by the intrigue, too."

"Another mystery trapped in a riddle, wrapped in an enigma."

"Something like that." Jonas ambled back to his clutter at the counter.

"But you never told anyone what you've been doing all these years. Not your family…Eddie had no idea. Your mother? They all thought you were…"

"Just a playboy bum." Jonas flashed that irresistible Gordon grin.

"But why?"

Jonas shrugged. "It's just easier. It's hard to explain and the *ins* and *outs* are pretty much off-limits. If I had a wife, I'd tell her." He winced, let out a weary laugh. "Of course if I had a wife, I never would have gotten into this in the first place. Think they call that irony."

"I'm well-acquainted with the concept." Eliza was back at the counter, standing next to Jonas.

"I'm sure you are."

Eliza and Jonas stared into each other's eyes, finally falling into each other's arms, sharing an interlude more powerful than a friendly hug, less intimate than a lovers' embrace.

"Wait," Eliza pulled away first. "That group, the one with those cryptic flyers, *The Quiet*…. They're part of this somehow, right?"

Jonas shook his head. "I can't…"

"They're connected to the Hackett murder?" Eliza licked her lips, tilted her head toward Jonas. "But how?"

"Really, I can't." Jonas smiled, took in Eliza's alluring beauty. "Not now. Not yet."

Chapter 24

"I'm sorry to tell you, kiddo, but schlepping tacky beach towels around town is part of your birthright. So you better get used to it!" Midge flipped her cell phone shut and sighed so loud it could be heard all the way across town at the Goodship Honda Labor Day Blow Out Sale where she expected Hannah to appear with a smile affixed to her sullen teenage face and a box of WSHP paraphernalia in her hands.

Eliza refilled Midge's glass with iced tea. It was almost three on Saturday afternoon. The crowd at Soup Opera—such as it was—had packed it in already; a good thing since Eliza had given both Dee Dee and Sam the day off to register for classes at Quimby College. Of course she was grateful to have Bert Santini for a few hours, but while she usually found his presence comforting, today was a bit awkward as Eliza was awash with guilt and confusion over her blossoming Jonas feelings. And to top it off, she'd have to wait until the end of September to get another dose of Dr. Sylvan's wisdom.

"Crazy weekend, huh?" Eliza knew the radio station's annual Labor Day Weekend Beach Blanket Bonanza wouldn't be the most exciting event this year. Something was going down with The Quiet. And maybe even the Hackett murder. And from what she'd overheard and what Jonas had said (or not said), Eliza was pretty sure it was going down this weekend.

"I can't wait for it to be over," Midge said, wiping her hand across her forehead like a melodramatic silent movie star. "Then I'm soaking in my tub for six days straight, eating bon bons and catching up on back issues of *The National Enquirer.* No kids. No husband. No radio nit wits."

"You say that every year. And you never make it. After the second day you start to prune."

"I don't care if I shrivel. Sell me to Sunkist and call it a day." Midge gulped her tea.

"It's particularly bad this year?"

Midge shifted her weight on the oversized stool, now sitting straight up like she had mounted a horse at the Kentucky Derby. "Where have you been the last two months?"

"It's tough, I know." Eliza was pretty sure now wasn't the time to share her new revelations with Midge. Especially since they were still so unformulated.

"Tough doesn't even begin to cover it."

"The mood at the station must be low."

"It's weird. Everyone seems so strange. Alex, Poppy, Robbie, Ashley…even that ancient mop top Sadie, they've all been walking around in a fog."

"It'll get better," Eliza said. "Give it time."

"And now Robbie went AWOL. Today of all days. Didn't even call in." Midge exhaled a disgusted breath.

"That doesn't sound like him. I thought he was so reliable."

"Yeah, well…"

"The poor kid must be taking it so hard. He was so close to Hackett."

"That's true, but I can't afford to coddle anyone today. That's why I enlisted her Royal Highness Princess Fancy Pants." Midge let out a laugh. "Everyone's gotta pull their weight. Eventually. I wish they'd just close the Hackett case already. That would help."

"I'm pretty sure it will happen soon."

"You know something." Midge's face brightened. "I can't believe you're holding out on me."

"I'm not." Eliza shook her head, played nervously with a menu.

"Oh, come on, Tom said something, didn't he? What gives?"

"Tom didn't say anything. Really." Eliza wasn't lying, but she felt another pang of something—maybe regret, maybe guilt—that any information or implications she may have had came from Jonas.

"Speak of the devil." Midge waved her hand as the chimes signaled Tom's entrance.

"Need some help with crowd control?" Tom chuckled as he surveyed the empty eatery.

"Hilarious, Chief," Midge jibed. "You obviously missed your calling. Caroline's has open mic nights every Monday."

"Hiding out, Midge? Dandy Dave and Hannah were looking for you down at Honda."

"Oh, what a relief. If Princess Fancy Pants made it, I don't have to rush over."

"Me and my big mouth." Tom shrugged, smiled at Eliza. "So we're still on for tonight, right?"

"You bet." Eliza returned the smile. "You want to go to the barbeque in Town Square and then maybe catch a movie? That new Brad Pitt's running at the Arts."

"Let's leave it up in the air for now."

"Another man intimidated by Brad Pitt," Midge joked.

"Brad's got nothing on me." Tom smiled broadly as he raised his arm in a muscleman pose. "I've just got to take care of something first. And I'm not sure how long it will take."

"Like what? Solving a murder, maybe?" Midge sighed.

"Everything in its own time."

"You sound awfully casual for a man with an unsolved murder on his hands."

"Well, worrying doesn't seem to help. Thought I'd try a new approach." Tom's voice was still buoyant, but his worried expression revealed his true mood.

"Now I see why you never auditioned for the Goodship Players," Eliza said, trying to keep the conversation light.

"Ah, everyone's a critic," Tom sighed. "Do me a favor: just go home and stay put. I'll call you."

"Okay."

"I mean it," Tom said, and Eliza could detect a new urgency in his voice. "Stay there and wait for my call."

"Yes, sir." Eliza offered a mock salute.

"Party like it's 1955," Midge laughed.

"In that case, I'll expect to hear a lot more Fats Domino and Bill Hailey and the Comets on WSHP."

"Rock around the clock, gramps." Midge returned Tom's wave as he exited Soup Opera.

"So what's with him?" Midge asked, now sprawling out in a booth.

"I figured something was going down this weekend."

"So you've been holding out. I knew it."

"Not really," Eliza said, flinging a rag. "But I'm pretty sure The Quiet is involved."

"The Quiet? You mean that wacky group with the cryptic flyers? I thought they were closing in on Hackett's murderer."

Eliza nodded. "I think it's all related."

"But how?"

"I haven't exactly put it together yet. But from what Jonas said…"

"Jonas, huh?" Midge's eyebrows lurched. "The plot thickens."

"Indeed it does. And right now it's about as thick and murky as my black bean soup."

****

"Better get our fill," Bonnie joked as she plunged her spoon into the steaming bowl of clam chowder. "If we're your only customers, guess you'll be closing up shop pretty soon." She laughed, exposing those neon bright white veneers.

"We're just late, is all," Zach said, getting comfortable at their little table by the window. He took a bite of the Cajun chicken wrap Eliza assembled with something less than zeal.

"We've been slow lately, but not *that* slow." Eliza laughed, exchanged a glance with Midge. She knew she'd have to work hard to like these two.

"Don't worry, it'll pick up big time next week when everyone's home from vacation," Midge said.

"Looks like a lot of folks are back already," Bonnie said. "We followed the radio station signs all the way out to the beach and up to the Honda place. And there were big crowds."

"Music to my ears." Midge let out a sigh of relief.

"And we weren't even looking for a car," Zach said, flashing his own neon bright veneers. "That's how effective your promotion is."

"Bright colors and balloons work every time. I don't care what the marketing experts say." Midge seemed to enjoy this new pair a lot more than Eliza did.

"Holy shitake mushroom!" Bonnie exclaimed.

"What?" Eliza and Midge's eyes met mid eye roll.

"That's the car!"

"Whoa...so it is," Zach nodded.

"What car?"

Midge and Eliza looked out the window watching Robbie Coates' two-toned orange and green vintage VW Beetle zoom down Pleasant Street.

"Go Speed Racer," Midge joked. "You're already way past late for work."

"That was the car we saw that night."

"In the radio station parking lot," Bonnie said, lowering her voice, even though no one besides Midge and Eliza were in the restaurant. "You know, the night that talk show shock jock guy was murdered."

"Are you sure?" Midge furrowed her brows.

"Yes. Zach commented on it, didn't you, Poodle?"

"I surely did. It looked just like the car my roomie had at UVA back in the hippy dippy '70's. Surprised to see one still zipping around."

"Are you sure it was the same night Hackett was killed?"

"Oh yes, it was our first night walking around. We'll never forget it. I mean given all the dramatic events and all."

"I'm surprised to see one still zipping around after all these years," Zach marveled as he watched Robbie careen up a side street.

"There won't be much longer if that fella's not careful," Bonnie chirped. "The way he's driving he could kill somebody."

"You can say that again," Midge said.

Chapter 25

The drive to the station was a lead-footed blur. "Making up for lost time," Midge called it, as though she didn't do the NASCAR nonsense every day. Midge wouldn't leave without Eliza. And Eliza couldn't close up shop before that new insidiously chipper couple with the neon veneers was ready to exit. And they weren't done before ordering take-out tubs of clam chowder and lobster bisque and cajoling Eliza into throwing together—with all the enthusiasm of a recidivist truant called to the principal's office—a Cajun turkey wrap for their son's dinner.

"They could be wrong, you know," Eliza said slamming on the imaginary emergency brake as Midge sped through a yellow light.

"You just don't like them." Midge smiled. "Which is actually sort of great."

"How is that great?"

"Because you like everybody."

"I don't like everybody. Ask Miriam Sussman."

"Well, Mother Theresa would be hard pressed to like that bitter old crank. But you definitely don't like Bonnie and Zach." Midge laughed.

"I don't know them enough to not like them...yet." Eliza grimaced. "But that's beside the point. The point is: they may have gotten the night wrong. Who knows when they really saw Robbie's car in the parking lot?"

"Okay, but it's worth checking out, right?"

"Not if we're dead on arrival."

"Broken record, grandma." Midge laughed as they pulled into the WSHP lot. "See, I always get you to your destination in one piece."

"Much obliged."

"Oh, great." Midge sprinted out of the Volvo as she saw Robbie barreling out of the station door, leaving the car vibrating from the high velocity journey with Eliza still precariously nestled in the passenger seat, her right foot throbbing from the imaginary emergency brake.

"Robbie! Wait!" Midge ran across the lot, her right tan Clark's comfort mule trailing behind her.

"What?" Robbie dropped a picture frame and a cassette tape before dashing into his two-tone orange and green vintage VW bug. "Yeah, I know: I'm fired, right?" Doesn't matter anymore anyway."

"No! Wait. Please." Midge picked up the frame and tape as Robbie floored the gas and took off out of the lot like Midge had been his Driver's Ed instructor.

Midge hobbled back to get her errant shoe then loped back to the car. "Jesus, will you look at this?" Midge tossed the picture frame at Eliza and the tape on the dashboard. She swung the Volvo into action.

"Whoa. Hold on!" Eliza grabbed the dashboard ledge and worked the imaginary brake. She fingered the cassette, looked at the label's child-like lettering: *Toxic* "Can we play this? There may be some clues."

"Wish we could," Midge sighed. "But my fancy car only has a CD player."

Eliza frowned, completely convinced if they couldn't hear the tape it most certainly contained everything they needed to solve the case. "What's this?" Eliza looked at the autographed photo of Paul Hackett. "You know, I don't think he was such a bad guy."

"Who?" Midge took a gamble and headed toward the Nature Center, following the windy back roads of Goodship like she was navigating a European race track.

"Hackett. He actually has a kind face. I think his whole act was just shtick, you know? I don't think he really meant any harm."

"You're priceless. Zach and Bonnie you can't stomach. But Hackett's just a clown."

"I'm not defending him. I'm just saying he wasn't such a menace." Eliza gritted her teeth as Midge dipped over a pothole. "Listen to the inscription: 'Tell the world to shove it where the sun don't shine. Loud and proud, kid. All day, every day, play to win!"

"You're right. He wasn't original enough to be dangerous." Midge snickered.

"Okay, I'm just...hey, where are we going?"

"Trust me. I think I know where he went."

They made the trek to the Nature Center, dashing along every curvy back road in Midge's leisurely escaped convict car-jacker dance. The summer had rushed by in a chaotic blur: so much had happened, yet nothing seemed clear. So much was left unresolved. And would remain so, Eliza feared, even after Hackett's murder had been solved.

They were closing in; on that, both women were sure.

Midge turned into the same long, winding road that led to the Nature Center, but instead of following it to the main parking lot like the day she and Eliza had dropped off Hannah's SAT study guide, she veered toward a woody bramble and pulled off onto a dusty alcove, well-worn by cars once filled with people— mostly teenagers—seeking romantic refuge.

"So this is where it all began," Eliza smiled as the two exited the car. "I can just imagine Gus having his way with you here."

"Only Gus?" Midge laughed. The maudlin memory of Hannah's sullen teenage rebuke at the Nature Center information hut was now mixed with her own teen reveries of late nights spent fighting off Johnny Wade and later Gus before succumbing to their awkward persuasion and her own adolescent urges while K.C. DePalma, the late night DJ her father would have axed had he known about his role in his daughter's fantasies, scrolled through the Top 40.

"You've been holding out."

"Takes one to know one."

"Oh, don't start," Eliza sighed. "I'm not. I mean, I don't know anything substantial."

"I like the way you sort of trailed off into a whisper at 'substantial.' A very clever and effective acting technique."

"Will you stop?" But it was Eliza who did just that—stopped dead in her tracks as she heard rustling.

"Probably just a raccoon or maybe a coyote," Midge said with confidence as she continued walking.

"Oh, great! Just what we need—a showdown with nature."

"Well, where do you think we are?" Midge laughed as they negotiated their way through a messy collection of leaves and branches and unkempt bushes separating the well-manicured Nature Center from a vast, wild, mysterious landscape.

"That's just what I was going to ask you."

"At least you didn't wear the wrong shoes," Midge said, gingerly stepping in her comfort clogs, eyeing Eliza's Rykas with more than a hint of envy. "This used to be the Winthrop Retreat Center," Midge said, as they approached a fountain, now covered with leaves and willowy fuzz.

"What was that? And what is it now?"

"Now, it's what it looks like. An abandoned playground for hormonal teenage antics."

"But it started out as something far grander, no?" Eliza knew it had to have been designed for spiritual pursuits by people with lofty ideals and the deep pockets to match. Its regal remnants: stone paths and sculpted gardens, now in disrepair, told the story. Or at least part of it. They walked by a huge copper sundial that reminded Eliza of the set of a movie about ancient Rome on which she had once worked.

"For years it was a well known center for spiritual and psychological retreats and workshops. A lot of prestigious teachers came here. People like Norman Vincent Peele, Louise Hay, even Deepak Chopra came before it suddenly closed."

"Wow. When did it close? Why?"

"About seventeen, maybe eighteen years now. It was before Hannah was born, I think. Long before you hit town, lady. Sorry, but it was a real scandal."

"Geez, I miss everything."

"It had been around for as long as I could remember. Founded back in the '50's, I think, by Cyrus Winthrop, heir to some sort of mining and banking fortunes. Really ahead of its time, offering all that human potential type garbage before EST came along in the '60's."

"*Garbage?* huh? Guess you're not a believer."

"Not so much. Anyway, it was still pretty impressive. Imagine all those brilliant people congregated in Goodship. Someone said Carl Jung gave a lecture here once."

"Impressive. Now get to the scandal part." Eliza's ankles were getting scratched up in the mélange of branches. While she wished she'd worn jeans instead of her light pink floral crop pants, she was grateful she wasn't wearing shorts.

"Now who's being dismissive?"

"I just figure we're headed this way for a reason, right? So I'd like to get to the finish line in time."

"Okay, so Drummond Winthrop, the son of Cyrus, went crazy, or so the story goes. He started writing letters to *The New York Times* and he'd stand in the middle of the town square yelling. Something about his father being a disciple of Satan. The last time anyone saw him he was in the band shell in the center of town screaming, 'No longer shall I speak the evil words of my father,' or some such blather. Then he cut out his tongue with a machete and bled to death."

"How awful. But why did they close down? I mean was it that much of a scandal to have a mentally ill son in the '90's?"

"No, of course not. The son's craziness was just the tip of the iceberg. But reporters started poking around and rumors floated about the place being run by a cult. By then Cyrus was old and sick and any outside funding dried up pretty fast. By the time he died, a few years later, the other kids—I think there was another son and a daughter—decided it wasn't worth maintaining."

"So they just let it go to seed."

"Pretty much."

"That's the real scandal."

"Spoken like a real nature girl."

"Well, I can appreciate beauty. In all its forms." Eliza laughed, then jumped back as a pair of squirrels scampered by.

"We'll have to come out here on Halloween." Midge laughed as she walked by a pond, dirty and lifeless.

"Slow down here." She walked slowly as she led Eliza past a formidable oak tree.

"We're closing in?"

"Indeed we are. Shhh.."

They quietly approached a secluded area shaped like a circle, with an abandoned fountain in the center. "They used to call this the Sacred Circle," Midge whispered. "It was the most popular meditation site at the Center."

Midge put her finger to her lips as they heard voices.

"God, there's no time for this. Get it together, man!"

"Wow," Eliza whispered as she spied two men. The guy talking was that weird guy, Carl, the one she and Midge had seen visiting Hannah at the Nature Center, the one who drove by her house with The Quiet flyers; the same guy she'd seen in Dr. Sylvan's office.

Midge's instincts were right on the money. The other guy was Robbie Coates.

"I can't. I just can't do this anymore," Robbie said, his arms flailing like an agitated cartoon character.

"Do what, boy? Call me in the middle of the night to finish your sacred duty?"

"What?" Midge and Eliza whispered, almost in unison. They stared incredulously at the two guys, then back at each other.

"Respect the Silence. Honor the Silence. Avenge the Silence." A voice bellowed over a loudspeaker, or maybe it was a megaphone. Eliza thought the voice, a woman's, powerful and entrancing, was strange, but somehow familiar. *Strangely familiar*, she thought as she followed Midge following Carl and Robbie toward the thunderous voice.

"Get a load of this!" Eliza blurted, muffling the sound with her hand clasped over her mouth. She stood with Midge at the edge of the scene, out of sight of the

small crowd of thirty or so—mostly young people—
gathered around the broken stone steps that surrounded
the once glorious house that must have been the
Retreat's main meeting hall. The followers, all rocking
back and forth, seemed hypnotically rapt by their
leader, a small woman shrouded in a flowing cranberry
and gold robe, a hood obstructing her face.

"Meet the Queen Bee?" Midge stood, hands on hips,
stifling a bemused laugh. Eliza was so astonished by the
whole business, she stood motionless her mouth agape.
They were standing at a pretty far distance, so Eliza
may have been imagining things when she thought she
recognized the cute, chubby girl who'd visited Jonas.
She figured the girl was some sort of mole, an agent of
good, working with Jonas to expose the cult, and
somehow having her there provided a sense of safety.
Or at least a sprinkle of sanity.

"Howard and Carl are passing out the suggestions.
Do with them as you see fit. Follow your deepest
conscience. But keep in mind: Monday is Labor Day.
Let the world hear our message, our work, loud and
clear." The woman's voice was pulsating, forceful,
unwavering. "And whatever you do, wherever you go,
don't forget our sacred mission."

"V.O.S. V.O.S," the crowd chanted like a bizarre
monotone football chant.

"Oh, God, so it was Robbie," Midge said clutching
Eliza's arm, pulling her back toward the deserted
Sacred Circle. "Looks like we just stumbled onto The
Quiet. And you were right; they were responsible for
Hackett's murder."

"I guess." Eliza was dumbfounded. "But how?
Why?"

"And what does V.O.S. mean?" The vision of the
deadly message on the studio glass with the mysterious
signature V.O.S. ran through Midge's mind.

"I don't know, maybe Vow of Silence?" Eliza shrugged. "I've never seen a cult up close. It's surreal." She was imagining Jonas' reaction when he went to rescue his girlfriend from the grips of another crazy group. It was a sad and strange feeling. *Strangely familiar?* Eliza was gripped by the unmistakable feeling that she was missing something so obvious and crucial. But what or who was she missing?

"If it was Vow of Silence, we wouldn't hear the chant. They'd be mouthing it. Or signing it." Midge let out a half-laugh as the chanting continued in the background. "V.O.S. V.O.S," followed by the guru's invocation, "Respect the Silence, Honor the Silence, Avenge the Silence."

"Maybe it's the Voice of Silence." Eliza rolled her eyes, regaining her jaded composure, if only for a moment.

"Oh, God, Hannah. She was friendly with that Carl guy. She was alone with him in the information office." Midge's words gushed out in a maternal panic. She was turning gray, looking clammy and shaking.

"She's okay, honey." Eliza grabbed her friend's shoulders. "That was last month. Hannah's nowhere near here. She's with Dandy Dave and Gus at the Honda remote. Remember?"

"Right. Right. You're right." Midge banished the instant terror from her mom brain. "Should we call Tom?" Midge started fumbling in her purse for her cell phone.

"Yeah. I guess." Eliza also scrambled for her phone. "And Jonas."

Suddenly there was silence. And then this from Midge: "Oh, God, no! This can't be good."

"What now? Having trouble getting service, too?" Eliza had wandered back near the big oak. She had punched in Jonas' number but she couldn't get a signal.

Then out of habit—or maybe it was a twinge of guilt—she tried Tom's number, also to no avail.

"Sorry ladies, you don't get very good reception out here." It was Carl, his face painted in his signature Kabuki white and now clad in a royal blue cape. He was also brandishing an ancient fencing sword, as were his compatriots, three other young men, each in vibrant capes. Red, yellow, purple. They looked like a cadre of swashbuckling crayons.

Carl and the red crayon grabbed Eliza's arms, yellow and purple encircled Midge. "It's a dead zone."

Chapter 26

"I am not a meddler!" Eliza protested as Midge laughed. Or maybe it was her mother doing the laughing. Or Miriam Sussman. Or Dr. Sylvan. "We won't tell anyone anything. Really, we don't even know." It was a strange sensation this dipping in and out of sleepy consciousness. One day ran into the next. Light fading, flirting with dark, darkness fighting the next wave of light. How many blurry cycles had she swirled through? Days plural, surely, maybe even a week's worth. Eliza doubted it had been months yet. *But what if it's already been years,* she thought as she started to drift again. *Who would help me?*

The crayons were there, pointing and poking their swords. Red, yellow, purple. And blue. Blue was the most dangerous. Blue held her down while that odd woman in the cranberry cape yelled at him, then her. *Strangely familiar.* They poked her, pouring the sleepy time potion into her veins. Now there was a new one: white. The white crayon poked her and it stung and felt icy cold like a soda gulped down too fast.

"I have to make my own decisions," Eliza said.

"It's too late for all that," the strange woman in the cranberry cape said. Or maybe it was Dr. Sylvan. But why was she dressed in such a bizarre outfit? And she looked mean. No, more like fierce. There was no hint of the kind, sagacious therapist who had once helped Eliza so much.

"But, please. Please."

"It's okay, sweetheart. Whatever you decide will be okay." It was Eddie now, gently rubbing her forehead. "It's your choice." But how could Eddie be here with her, so real, smelling like earth and peppermint Lifesavers and Irish Spring? Had Eliza died? Maybe dying was drifting in and out, blurry and fuzzy spinning through your life until you were ready to leave it all behind.

"But I'm not ready," Eliza said. "I'm not done yet!" Eliza thought she was shouting, but no one heard her. No one was listening. Then the crayons were agitated, poking her again and again with their swords. Dr. Sylvan shook her and yelled at the blue Carl crayon. "It's not enough. You didn't give her enough. Stupid, stupid boy."

"Please. I'm sorry. I won't say anything. But I'm not done." Eliza shouted. "I'm still here!"

"She's coming around," the white crayon said, tapping her gently on the shoulder. Eliza breathed deeply, took in the powerful scent of disinfectant.

Eliza opened her eyes; she saw the tubes in her arm, the white walls. "How did I get here?"

"It's okay, honey. You're in the hospital," the nurse said. "You've been here for four days."

"Midge? Is Midge okay?"

"You're friend? From the radio?"

Eliza nodded.

"She's fine honey." The nurse raised Eliza's bed. "You'll be fine too."

****

"So it was Dr. Sylvan?" Eliza shook her head.

"I told you Sunny Sylvan was loop de doo. Big time." Midge laughed.

"Wait, you two know her?" Tom asked.

"Apparently not," Eliza said giving Midge that lock your lips and throw away the key look, as Tom

continued recounting the shakedown of The Quiet.
Beryl Sylvan, it seemed, was the daughter of Cyrus
Winthrop. She had started the group as a way to reclaim
her father's good name and eradicate all the toxic things
said about him by her brother Drummond and later,
investigative reporters.

The Quiet had been operating for several years as an
introspective group, with members instructed on
personal values, the fulcrum of which was limited
speech. "It spiraled out of control; in the last year or
two, when Dr. Sylvan decided it wasn't enough to not
say anything 'toxic,' Tom explained. "Members also
had to now take 'responsible action' against those who
'spewed toxins into society.'"

"Wow. So she told Robbie to kill Hackett?"

"And that woman in Chicago? The cable host who
was shot when Gus was there?" Midge asked.

"That needs to be sorted out," Tom said. "I'm sure
she'll deny it. Probably claim she never instructed
anyone to do anything. That's how these cult cowards
usually operate. Ask Jonas, it's his area."

"Is he okay? Was he there?"

"Yeah, he's fine. You can thank Ethan and that girl,
Cassie, for getting you here in time."

"Ethan? He was working with Jonas?"

"Apparently." Midge laughed. "I know it shocked
me, too, but there's someone in my family who can
actually keep his mouth shut."

"But what did they give me…us…and how come
you're okay?"

"It was a potent cocktail of valium, Xanax and anti-
freeze."

"That explains the sickeningly sweet taste. But how
come you're up and around and I was in a coma?"

"I don't think you were under long enough to
officially call it a coma, drama queen," Midge laughed,

stroking Eliza's arm. "And I was out for a few hours. Guess they didn't give me as much. Or maybe I have a better tolerance."

"Guess I better get out more."

"Not so fast, slugger," Tom said, petting her cheek. "I was thinking just the opposite."

"Wait 'til you see *The Grapevine*."

"That cyber rag's back in business?"

"Yep, and Miriam...or her grandson...is bending over backwards to be the town's PR firm. You should see the puff piece they wrote about us." Midge chortled.

"Much to Detective Duckheimer's chagrin." Tom let out a sigh.

"I'll bet," Eliza said with a weak laugh. "I'm surprised he's not staked outside my room."

"Think she's well enough to know?" Midge asked Tom.

"Know what? Tell me."

"Hmm... I'm not sure." Tom shook his head.

"Tell me already."

"Okay, tell, her."

"Your mother," Midge said.

"You didn't."

"Sorry." Midge said, licking her lips. "Honey, I had to call her. You were in a coma."

"I thought you just said I wasn't under long enough."

"Well, she's here. Sat by your bedside for nearly two days,"

"We made her take a break just about twenty minutes ago."

"Sent her down to the cafeteria."

"Where she's no doubt casting for some hideous low-rent medical drama." Eliza sighed, bracing herself for Margot.

And just then Eliza's head started throbbing as she heard the sound of her mother's ambitious stilettos. And Detective Duckheimer's rubber-soled quacking.

"Isn't this man marvelous?" Margot breezed into the room with Detective Duckheimer close behind. "Really, Detective, have you ever thought about moving to Hollywood? I could get you work like that." Margot snapped her brightly manicured fingers. The pink nails, the fuchsia blouse clashed with her new Lucille Ball ersatz red hair. She rubbed Duckheimer's shoulder.

Duckheimer snorted, moved to the window. "Detective Duckheimer isn't much of a movie fan," Tom said apologetically, as Margot brushed his cheek with an air kiss.

"Oh, how unfortunate." Margot turned her attention to Eliza, depositing a quick peck on her daughter's forehead.

"Hi Mom," Eliza said.

"I'm so glad to see you awake, darling."

"And confined to bed," Duckheimer added with a scowl.

"As soon as you get out of here, we can discuss the new project. Have I got a come-back part for you!"

Eliza smiled, waiting for sweet sleep to relieve her from this latest trauma. "Thanks, Midge. For everything."

Chapter 27

Chicken noodle soup from a can, the manic clacking of Margot's neo-maternal stilettos and an incessant loop of *The Smoking Gun*, that infamous tape, the one found on Midge's dashboard, which had been leaked, without Detective Duckheimer's consent, to the media, added a certain salty irony to Eliza's convalescence.

She couldn't resist watching the cable coverage. A particularly smarmy show called *21st Century Crime Watch* played the tape constantly, offering an array of legal and pop psych hucksters' analyses. The show even had a countdown clock to Robbie and Carl's preliminary hearings in the corner of the screen.

Eliza and Margot enjoyed a perverse bonding over the show's sleazy highlight: cheesy re-enactment scenes with low rent actors using the actual tape's transcript.

"It's playing again?" Margot feigned annoyance as she delivered Eliza's lunch: vegetable soup Dee Dee had dropped off from Soup Opera.

"Every hour on the hour," Eliza sighed. She'd never admit she actually missed the Campbell's soup Margot had served for the first few days when people were still politely giving Eliza her space. Somehow the canned offering conjured the warmest childhood feeling she could muster; reminiscent, Eliza guessed, of the few times her mother had actually comforted her when she was a girl.

"Oh, here," Margot said, plopping a sleeve of saltines on the bed as she snuggled in next to Eliza, ready for the 2 PM showing.

Robbie: (*wielding a knife*) Why'd you have to be like him?"

Hackett: What? Whoa. What are you doing? That's some Boy Scout knife you got there. Be careful, kid."

Robbie: It's too late for that.

　(*Robbie lunging closer to Hackett*)

Hackett: Come on, kid. Really, what is this? Some sort of sick joke? It's not funny.

　Robbie: No, it's not. Why'd you have to be like him?

Hackett: Like who? What are you talking about?

Robbie: My bastard father. You're just like him. You hurt people. You know you do. Words have power, Paul.

Hackett: It's a gig, kid; that's all. Just an act. You know that…. Whoa, watch it. (*Trying to dislodge knife out of Robbie's hand*) …Come on, it's your ticket out, too!

Robbie: No. Not this way. It's wrong 'The B' said so.

Hackett: 'The B?' You're involved with that Quiet crap?

Robbie: It's not crap. It's… (*crying*) Christ, I can't. (*Knife falls to floor. Hackett scrambles to pick up. Carl Whelan bursts in studio.*)

Carl: What's taking so long? For God's sake, do your duty, dude. Come on!"

Robbie: No, Carl, please. We can't. Really, we can't!

Hackett: (*w/ Robbie shaking and Carl pushing him into studio console*) What the…who's this circus freak?

Carl:*(grabbing headphones hanging on Hackett's neck, pulling cord tight)* The Circus is over, Mr. Hackett. You're over!

(Hackett struggles, gasps, makes gurgling noises until he slumps lifeless over console.)

Robbie: No, God, no!

(Rustling noise and the tape clicks off)

"Simply riveting," Margot said. "We'll have to watch it again."

"Stick around. They'll roll it again at three."

"You know this would make a great TV movie."

"I'm sure Lifetime's already all over it." Eliza huddled under the covers, clutching Arbuckle and the saltines, knowing what was coming next.

"You don't want to get gypped out of a credit."

"Really, Mom, it's okay."

"Nonsense! You could play yourself!" Margot pulled out a cell phone from her burgundy retro *Maude* vest. "I'm sure you can pull that off. I'll make some calls."

Almost on cue Eliza's phone rang.

"Ah, see what I tell you? They're calling you!" Margot was beaming.

Eliza shook her head, laughed as she spied the caller ID. "Don't get carried away, it's just Midge."

"Oh, thanks a lot!" Midge snickered.

"So glad you called."

"Fun and games with Margot?"

"Non-stop. So how's it going out there in the real world?'

"She swears nothing happened." Midge was referring to her latest obsession: getting to the bottom of Poppy's alleged affair with Hackett.

"Maybe nothing did. What does Alex think?"

"He's choosing to believe her."

"Sounds like there's still a little tension there."

"Just a little. What can you do?"

"Do you believe her?"

"I don't know. She says they had a deep 'soul connection.'

"Wow."

"Yeah, so what can you say to that?"

"Guess obnoxious waters run deep."

"Oh, here we go."

"I'm just saying you never know. That's all." Eliza sighed, watched her mother preening in front of the mirror. What—*or who*—was she trying to impress? For a second, visions of Margot and Detective Duckheimer flashed through Eliza's mind with an amalgam of dread and amusement. "What about Declan?"

"Oh, didn't I mention he and Poppy are now joined at the hip?"

"And this doesn't bother Alex?"

"No, I thought you were getting that gaydar fixed." Midge laughed. "Guess they reminisce about Hackett's deep soul."

"Come on, Midge. Just because we didn't see it doesn't mean it wasn't there. Everyone has many layers."

"Maybe so, but if you keep pulling back the layers on Paul Hackett's onion, you'll go home stinking to high heaven."

"So who asked you to go peeling?"

"Touché." Midge chuckled. "Oh, cripes!"

"What's wrong?" Eliza heard crashing noises and loud voices in the background.

"Sadie Weber's running down the hall hysterical. I think the computer system knocked us off the air again. Either that or someone ate Sadie's last red velvet cupcake."

"Well you better go fix whatever it is."

"Guess so. I hope I can figure out how to blame whatever it is on Sadie. I'm in the mood to wield the ax."

"Big talk, lady. Later." Eliza smiled. She was feeling better. In another week—even sooner, if the doctor gave her the go-ahead—she could head back to Soup Opera and reclaim her life.

"I like Midge," Margot said, sitting on the foot of the bed.

"Me, too."

"She's spunky. You two have a cute friendship going. Very Thelma and Louise."

Eliza shook her head. "Not so sure that's such a great example. Besides that whole crime spree business, it didn't exactly end well."

"True enough." Margot sighed. "They really missed the boat on that one, didn't they?"

Eliza laughed, knowing exactly what her mother was getting at. "Yep, no sequels."

Chapter 28

"Ain't that a kick in the head?" Oscar Oleo said, punching the local newspaper at the Soup Opera counter. "Can you believe this Sylvan dame is pleading 'diminished mental capacity'?"

"Well, maybe all those years listening to people's problems pushed her over the edge," quipped Georgia Rhodes as she plunged her spoon into a steaming bowl of cream of mushroom.

"Shrinks!" Oscar laughed. "They're all nuts!"

"You know she was a therapist for over thirty years. She helped a lot of people," Lois Danziger said as she nervously grabbed the last stool at the end of the crowded counter. "People shouldn't be so judgmental."

With that, Lois' daughter, Dee Dee, let out an audible chortle, slammed shut her *Abnormal Psychology* text and dashed into the kitchen to fetch bowls of crab bisque and smoky pea for Chief Tom Santini and Detective Duckheimer.

It had been four weeks since the secrets of Dr. Sylvan and The Quiet were exposed and Goodship was swinging back into its normal routines and rhythms.

Robbie Coates had been charged, along with Carl Whelan, with Paul Hackett's murder; but Felicia Downes a noted attorney famous for insanity defenses had signed on to represent Robbie *pro bono*. And Dan Coates, Robbie's long absent and much maligned father, had re-surfaced, pleading his son's case on various TV shows. Robbie's shaky accusations against his idol as well as his desperate pleas to Carl to put the kibosh on the deadly plan might be used to mitigate the troubled young producer's sentence. Whelan, who it turned out, was Beryl Sylvan's son, had refused to enter a plea and was under observation at the state mental hospital where his mother was also undergoing tests. So far, Dr. Sylvan had only been charged with the attempted murders of Eliza and Midge.

And from the reactions, Eliza and Midge figured a lot of folks in town had been patients of Dr. Sylvan's at one time or other. Lois, for sure. And Poppy, who'd been acting skittish since the Hackett murder, practically fainted at the news. She was now huddled with Declan Rinaldi in their new regular spot in a back booth, exchanging soulful looks and hushed tones, which no one, including Alex, found in the least bit threatening.

"Too bad they can't nail her on mind-control charges," Midge said as she swiped a few curly fries from Lois' plate.

"I thought we were staying out if it." Eliza laughed as she refilled Midge's iced tea.

"It's a little late for that, I'd say, Mrs. Gordon." Detective Duckheimer shuffled to the counter in search of oyster crackers.

"Better late than never?" Eliza smiled, tossed Duckheimer two packets of crackers. She was in a jovial mood. After leaving the hospital and recuperating, for two weeks at the Gordon Family Museum—with both her mother and Jonas waiting on her—Eliza finally moved into her new Briar Ridge townhouse. Margot praised her daughter's new digs with her usual charm: "Well, it's good to travel light. When you're *finally* ready to move back to Hollywood, you won't have much to pack."

Fortunately after three weeks, Margot's maternal obligations were eschewed in favor of an emergency trip to Hawaii where her boy-toy protégé Rex Manaway was summoned for an audition for a yet unsigned remake of *Magnum, P.I.*

"I'm glad to see everything's up and running at full speed," Jonas said as he approached the counter, eyeing the place for empty seats and smiling at Eliza.

"I'm moving them out as fast as I can, professor," Eliza said, returning his irresistible crooked Gordon grin with a wink. Jonas would be staying on in Goodship, at least for a while; he'd signed on to teach a course called The Psychology and Sociology of Cults at Quimby College. Eliza wasn't sure if a new found interest or the dishy teacher had sparked Dee Dee to take the class.

Jonas placed an order for clam chowder as Tom and Duckheimer beckoned him to their booth.

Bonnie, half of the insipid couple with the neon bright veneers riding solo on a Thursday afternoon, was shut out of her window table. But that didn't deter her from ordering her favorite lobster bisque. "Well, I guess I had nothing to worry about," she said as she straddled the stool Oscar Oleo just vacated with his signature dismissive grunt. "You were right, Midge, this place is hopping."

Midge smiled and waved, giving Eliza a knowing glance. "So now that you're settled in, how do you like our sleepy little hamlet?"

"It's positively *divine,*" Bonnie said, her voice now lacquered in convenient Southern Comfort. "But there's nothing sleepy about Goodship. It's been nothing but exciting since day one."

"Give it a chance. It can get positively drowsy," Eliza said as she poked the dozing Jill Dondi on the arm.

"What? Oh, sorry, girlie," Jill said, shaking her head and adjusting the mammoth collar on her purple and yellow retro sixties blouse. "I've been up late every night going over my briefs." Jill, who was suing Miriam Sussman and her grandson for defamation, took an online legal course and, against the advice of everyone she knew, was acting as her own attorney.

"Since they locked up that crazy therapist, I wonder what all her patients will do." Bonnie smacked her lips. "I'd prescribe this bisque. It'll cure anything."

"Well, thank you kindly," Eliza said. She was going to have to give Bonnie the serious benefit of the doubt. Whether she liked it or not.

"I suppose folks will just have to take their own counsel," Midge said. "You know listen to your inner voice."

"But be *quiet* about it." Eliza and Midge laughed.

"No sense in letting other people tell you what to do, I always say," Bonnie said. "It's your life, stop talking about it and go out and live it."

"Wise words," Midge said, elbowing Eliza as both Tom and Jonas walked to the register.

"Indeed," Eliza said, sauntering to meet the men who currently occupied her heart and mind. "And you never know just how interesting it might get."

Soup Opera's Recipes

Soup Opera's Quiet as a Clam Chowder
  8 oz. fresh clams chopped or 6 oz. canned clams (w/
    juice)
  5 cups bottled clam juice
  1 cup flour
  1 cup white onion, finely chopped
  10 slices cooked bacon (optional)
  2 tablespoons butter
  4 med. potatoes, cooked & chopped into bite-sized chunks
  ½ cup milk
  ½ cup light cream
  1 teaspoon sea salt
  Cracked black pepper to taste

Preparation:
Heat the clam juice in a large saucepan on medium
heat. In a separate pan, melt butter and sauté the diced
onions until they appear translucent. Add bacon
(optional) and flour to the melted butter and stir
continuously for 5 minutes. Increase heat on clam juice
to medium-high, and, with a wire whisk, add flour,
butter and onion mixture to the liquid. Stir constantly,
breaking up any lumps that form. Add clams and stir.
Add potato chunks, milk, cream and salt, and continue
stirring. Decrease heat to medium-low and allow
chowder to simmer for 20-30 minutes, stirring
frequently to avoid burning or sticking. If chowder
becomes too thick add water or clam juice to achieve
desired consistency. Serve hot with oyster crackers,
adding freshly ground black pepper & sea salt to taste.

Eliza Gordon's 'Healthy' Killer Cajun Chicken Wraps
  3 tablespoons Cajun seasoning
  1 tablespoon flour
  1 teaspoon paprika
  12 oz. boneless, skinless chicken breast, cut into strips
  4 medium tortillas
  1/2 small red onion, thinly sliced
  2 cups mixed field greens, arugula, spinach or your
    choice of lettuces
  4 teaspoons low-fat mayonnaise or low-fat Ranch
    dressing
  1 teaspoon lemon juice
  4 oz. cheese (optional); choose cheddar, American or
    for extra zing pepper Jack.

Preparation:
Combine 3 tablespoons seasoning mix, flour, and paprika. Season chicken with salt and pepper and dredge in seasoning mixture. Coat a large, nonstick pan with cooking spray. Over medium-high heat, add chicken to pan, sautéing until cooked through, about 1 to 2 minutes per side. Remove chicken from heat and set aside. Combine mayonnaise (or Ranch dressing), lemon juice and 1/2 teaspoon Cajun seasoning for dressing. On each tortilla, spread 1 teaspoon dressing; add onion slices and greens. Top with chicken pieces (approximately two per tortilla) and cheese (optional) and wrap. Serves 4.

ABOUT THE AUTHOR

 Amy Beth Arkawy is the author of *Killing Time: An Eliza Gordon Mystery* and several plays including: *Psychic Chicken Soup* (McLaren Comedy Award nominee); *Full Moon, Saturday Night; Listening to Insomnia: Rage Amongst Yourselves; Crazy Vivian Doesn't Shop at Bloomie's Anymore, The Lost Mertz* and *The Postman Always Writes Twice*. Her work has been produced in New York City and across the country and featured in several anthologies. She is also a creativity coach/writing teacher, radio talk show host and freelance journalist. *Dead Silent* is the second in the Eliza Gordon mystery series.